Kilmeny of the Orchard

LUCY MAUD MONTGOMERY

Published in 1909

TABLE OF CONTENTS

DEDICATION

TO MY COUSIN BEATRICE A. MCINTYRE THIS BOOK IS
AFFECTIONATELY DEDICATED

"Kilmeny looked up with a lovely grace,
But nae smile was seen on Kilmeny's face;
As still was her look, and as still was her ee,
As the stillness that lay on the emerant lea,
Or the mist that sleeps on a waveless sea.
. . . .
Such beauty bard may never declare,
For there was no pride nor passion there;
. . . .
Her seymar was the lily flower,
And her cheek the moss-rose in the shower;
And her voice like the distant melodye
That floats along the twilight sea."

— The Queen's Wake
JAMES HOGG

THE THOUGHTS OF YOUTH

The sunshine of a day in early spring, honey pale and honey sweet, was showering over the red brick buildings of Queenslea College and the grounds about them, throwing through the bare, budding maples and elms, delicate, evasive etchings of gold and brown on the paths, and coaxing into life the daffodils that were peering greenly and perkily up under the windows of the co-eds' dressing-room.

A young April wind, as fresh and sweet as if it had been blowing over the fields of memory instead of through dingy streets, was purring in the tree-tops and whipping the loose tendrils of the ivy network which covered the front of the main building. It was a wind that sang of many things, but what it sang to each listener was only what was in that listener's heart. To the college students who had just been capped and diplomad by "Old Charlie," the grave president of Queenslea, in the presence of an admiring throng of parents and sisters, sweethearts and friends, it sang, perchance, of glad hope and shining success and high achievement. It sang of the dreams of youth that may never be quite fulfilled, but are well worth the dreaming for all that. God help the man who has never known such dreams—who, as he leaves his alma mater, is not already rich in aerial castles, the proprietor of many a spacious estate in Spain. He has missed his birthright.

The crowd streamed out of the entrance hall and scattered over the campus, fraying off into the many streets beyond. Eric Marshall and David Baker walked away together. The former had graduated in Arts that day at the head of his class; the latter had come to see the graduation, nearly bursting with pride in Eric's success.

Between these two was an old and tried and enduring friendship, although David was ten years older than Eric, as the mere tale of years goes, and a hundred years older in knowledge of the struggles and difficulties of life which age a man far more quickly and effectually than the passing of time.

7

Physically the two men bore no resemblance to one another, although they were second cousins. Eric Marshall, tall, broad-shouldered, sinewy, walking with a free, easy stride, which was somehow suggestive of reserve strength and power, was one of those men regarding whom less-favoured mortals are tempted seriously to wonder why all the gifts of fortune should be showered on one individual. He was not only clever and good to look upon, but he possessed that indefinable charm of personality which is quite independent of physical beauty or mental ability. He had steady, grayish-blue eyes, dark chestnut hair with a glint of gold in its waves when the sunlight struck it, and a chin that gave the world assurance of a chin. He was a rich man's son, with a clean young manhood behind him and splendid prospects before him. He was considered a practical sort of fellow, utterly guiltless of romantic dreams and visions of any sort.

"I am afraid Eric Marshall will never do one quixotic thing," said a Queenslea professor, who had a habit of uttering rather mysterious epigrams, "but if he ever does it will supply the one thing lacking in him."

David Baker was a short, stocky fellow with an ugly, irregular, charming face; his eyes were brown and keen and secretive; his mouth had a comical twist which became sarcastic, or teasing, or winning, as he willed. His voice was generally as soft and musical as a woman's; but some few who had seen David Baker righteously angry and heard the tones which then issued from his lips were in no hurry to have the experience repeated.

He was a doctor—a specialist in troubles of the throat and voice—and he was beginning to have a national reputation. He was on the staff of the Queenslea Medical College and it was whispered that before long he would be called to fill an important vacancy at McGill.

He had won his way to success through difficulties and drawbacks which would have daunted most men. In the year Eric was born David Baker was an errand boy in the big department store of Marshall and Company. Thirteen years later he graduated with high honors from Queenslea Medical College. Mr. Marshall had given him all the help which David's sturdy pride could be induced to accept, and now he insisted on sending the young man abroad for a post-graduate course in London and Germany. David Baker had eventually repaid every cent Mr. Marshall had expended on him; but he never ceased to cherish a passionate gratitude to the kind and generous man; and he loved that man's son with a love surpassing that of brothers.

He had followed Eric's college course with keen, watchful interest. It was his wish that Eric should take up the study of law or medicine now that he was through Arts; and he was greatly disappointed that Eric should have finally made up his mind to go into business with his father.

"It's a clean waste of your talents," he grumbled, as they walked home from the college. "You'd win fame and distinction in law—that glib tongue of yours was meant for a lawyer and it is sheer flying in the face of Providence to devote it to commercial uses—a flat crossing of the purposes of destiny. Where is your ambition, man?"

"In the right place," answered Eric, with his ready laugh. "It is not your kind, perhaps, but there is room and need for all kinds in this lusty young country of ours. Yes, I am going into the business. In the first place, it has been father's cherished desire ever since I was born, and it would hurt him pretty badly if I backed out now. He wished me to take an Arts course because he believed that every man should have as liberal an education as he can afford to get, but now that I have had it he wants me in the firm."

"He wouldn't oppose you if he thought you really wanted to go in for something else."

"Not he. But I don't really want to—that's the point, David, man. You hate a business life so much yourself that you can't get it into your blessed noddle that another man might like it. There are many lawyers in the world—too many, perhaps—but there are never too many good honest men of business, ready to do clean big things for the betterment of humanity and the upbuilding of their country, to plan great enterprises and carry them through with brain and courage, to manage and control, to aim high and strike one's aim. There, I'm waxing eloquent, so I'd better stop. But ambition, man! Why, I'm full of it—it's bubbling in every pore of me. I mean to make the department store of Marshall and Company famous from ocean to ocean. Father started in life as a poor boy from a Nova Scotian farm. He has built up a business that has a provincial reputation. I mean to carry it on. In five years it shall have a maritime reputation, in ten, a Canadian. I want to make the firm of Marshall and Company stand for something big in the commercial interests of Canada. Isn't that as honourable an ambition as trying to make black seem white in a court of law, or discovering some new disease with a harrowing name to torment poor creatures who might otherwise die peacefully in blissful ignorance of what ailed them?"

"When you begin to make poor jokes it is time to stop arguing with you," said David, with a shrug of his fat shoulders. "Go your own gait and dree your own weird. I'd as soon expect success in trying to storm the citadel single-handed as in trying to turn you from any course about which you had once made up your mind. Whew, this street takes it out of a fellow! What could have possessed our ancestors to run a town up the side of a hill? I'm not so slim and active as I was on MY graduation day ten years ago. By the way, what a lot of co-eds were in your class—twenty, if I counted right. When I graduated there were only two ladies in our class and they were the pioneers of their sex at Queenslea. They were well past their first youth, very grim and angular and serious; and they could never have been on speaking terms with a mirror in their best days. But mark you, they were excellent females—oh, very excellent. Times have changed with a vengeance, judging from the line-up of co-eds to-day. There was one girl there who can't be a day over eighteen—and she looked as if she were made out of gold and roseleaves and dewdrops."

"The oracle speaks in poetry," laughed Eric. "That was Florence Percival, who led the class in mathematics, as I'm a living man. By many she is considered the beauty of her class. I can't say that such is my opinion. I don't greatly care for that blonde, babyish style of loveliness—I prefer Agnes Campion. Did you notice her—the tall, dark girl with the ropes of hair and a sort of crimson, velvety bloom on her face, who took honours in philosophy?"

"I DID notice her," said David emphatically, darting a keen side glance at his friend. "I noticed her most particularly and critically—for someone whispered her name behind me and coupled it with the exceedingly interesting information that Miss Campion was supposed to be the future Mrs. Eric Marshall. Whereupon I stared at her with all my eyes."

"There is no truth in that report," said Eric in a tone of annoyance. "Agnes and I are the best of friends and nothing more. I like and admire her more than any woman I know; but if the future Mrs. Eric Marshall exists in the flesh I haven't met her yet. I haven't even started out to look for her—and don't intend to for some years to come. I have something else to think of," he concluded, in a tone of contempt, for which anyone might have known he would be punished sometime if Cupid were not deaf as well as blind.

"You'll meet the lady of the future some day," said David dryly. "And in spite of your scorn I venture to predict that if fate doesn't bring her before long you'll very soon start out to look for her. A word of advice, oh, son of your mother. When you go courting take your common sense with you."

"Do you think I shall be likely to leave it behind?" asked Eric amusedly.

"Well, I mistrust you," said David, sagely wagging his head. "The Lowland Scotch part of you is all right, but there's a Celtic streak in you, from that little Highland grandmother of yours, and when a man has that there's never any knowing where it will break out, or what dance it will lead him, especially when it comes to this love-making business. You are just as likely as not to lose your head over some little fool or shrew for the sake of her outward favour and make yourself miserable for life. When you pick you a wife please remember that I shall reserve the right to pass a candid opinion on her."

"Pass all the opinions you like, but it is MY opinion, and mine only, which will matter in the long run," retorted Eric.

"Confound you, yes, you stubborn offshoot of a stubborn breed," growled David, looking at him affectionately. "I know that, and that is why I'll never feel at ease about you until I see you married to the right sort of a girl. She's not hard to find. Nine out of ten girls in this country of ours are fit for kings' palaces. But the tenth always has to be reckoned with."

"You are as bad as Clever Alice in the fairy tale who worried over the future of her unborn children," protested Eric.

"Clever Alice has been very unjustly laughed at," said David gravely. "We doctors know that. Perhaps she overdid the worrying business a little, but she was perfectly right in principle. If people worried a little more about their unborn children—at least, to the extent of providing a proper heritage, physically, mentally, and morally, for them—and then stopped worrying about them after they ARE born, this world would be a very much pleasanter place to live in, and the human race would make more progress in a generation than it has done in recorded history."

"Oh, if you are going to mount your dearly beloved hobby of heredity I am not going to argue with you, David, man. But as for the matter of urging me to hasten and marry me a wife, why don't you"—It was on Eric's lips to say, "Why don't you get married to a girl of the right sort yourself and set me a good example?" But he checked himself. He knew that there was an old sorrow in David Baker's life which was not to be unduly jarred by the jests even of privileged friendship. He changed his question to, "Why don't you leave this on the knees of the gods where it properly belongs? I thought you were a firm believer in predestination, David."

"Well, so I am, to a certain extent," said David cautiously. "I believe, as an excellent old aunt of mine used to say, that what is to be will be and what isn't to be happens sometimes. And it is precisely such unchancy happenings that make the scheme of things go wrong. I dare say you think me an old fogy, Eric; but I know something more of the world than you do, and I believe, with Tennyson's Arthur, that 'there's no more subtle master under heaven than is the maiden passion for a maid.' I want to see you safely anchored to the love of some good woman as soon as may be, that's all. I'm rather sorry Miss Campion isn't your lady of the future. I liked her looks, that I did. She is good and strong and true—and has the eyes of a woman who could love in a way that would be worth while. Moreover, she's well-born, well-bred, and well-educated—three very indispensable things when it comes to choosing a woman to fill your mother's place, friend of mine!"

"I agree with you," said Eric carelessly. "I could not marry any woman who did not fulfill those conditions. But, as I have said, I am not in love with Agnes Campion—and it wouldn't be of any use if I were. She is as good as engaged to Larry West. You remember West?"

"That thin, leggy fellow you chummed with so much your first two years in Queenslea? Yes, what has become of him?"

"He had to drop out after his second year for financial reasons. He is working his own way through college, you know. For the past two years he has been teaching school in some out-of-the-way place over in Prince Edward Island. He isn't any too well, poor fellow—never was very strong and has studied remorselessly. I haven't heard from him since February. He said then that he was afraid he wasn't going to be able to stick it out till the end of the school year. I hope Larry won't break down. He is a fine fellow and worthy even of Agnes Campion. Well, here we are. Coming in, David?"

"Not this afternoon—haven't got time. I must mosey up to the North End to see a man who has got a lovely throat. Nobody can find out what is the matter. He has puzzled all the doctors. He has puzzled me, but I'll find out what is wrong with him if he'll only live long enough."

A LETTER OF DESTINY

Eric, finding that his father had not yet returned from the college, went into the library and sat down to read a letter he had picked up from the hall table. It was from Larry West, and after the first few lines Eric's face lost the absent look it had worn and assumed an expression of interest.

"I am writing to ask a favour of you, Marshall," wrote West. "The fact is, I've fallen into the hands of the Philistines—that is to say, the doctors. I've not been feeling very fit all winter but I've held on, hoping to finish out the year.

"Last week my landlady—who is a saint in spectacles and calico—looked at me one morning at the breakfast table and said, VERY gently, 'You must go to town to-morrow, Master, and see a doctor about yourself.'

"I went and did not stand upon the order of my going. Mrs. Williamson is She-Who-Must-Be-Obeyed. She has an inconvenient habit of making you realize that she is exactly right, and that you would be all kinds of a fool if you didn't take her advice. You feel that what she thinks to-day you will think to-morrow.

"In Charlottetown I consulted a doctor. He punched and pounded me, and poked things at me and listened at the other end of them; and finally he said I must stop work 'immejutly and to onct' and hie me straightway to a climate not afflicted with the north-east winds of Prince Edward Island in the spring. I am not to be allowed to do any work until the fall. Such was his dictum and Mrs. Williamson enforces it.

"I shall teach this week out and then the spring vacation of three weeks begins. I want you to come over and take my place as pedagogue in the Lindsay school for the last week in May and the month of June. The school year ends then and there will be plenty of teachers looking for the place, but just now I cannot get a suitable substitute. I have a couple of pupils who are

13

preparing to try the Queen's Academy entrance examinations, and I don't like to leave them in the lurch or hand them over to the tender mercies of some third-class teacher who knows little Latin and less Greek. Come over and take the school till the end of the term, you petted son of luxury. It will do you a world of good to learn how rich a man feels when he is earning twenty-five dollars a month by his own unaided efforts!

"Seriously, Marshall, I hope you can come, for I don't know any other fellow I can ask. The work isn't hard, though you'll likely find it monotonous. Of course, this little north-shore farming settlement isn't a very lively place. The rising and setting of the sun are the most exciting events of the average day. But the people are very kind and hospitable; and Prince Edward Island in the month of June is such a thing as you don't often see except in happy dreams. There are some trout in the pond and you'll always find an old salt at the harbour ready and willing to take you out cod-fishing or lobstering.

"I'll bequeath you my boarding house. You'll find it comfortable and not further from the school than a good constitutional. Mrs. Williamson is the dearest soul alive; and she is one of those old-fashioned cooks who feed you on feasts of fat things and whose price is above rubies.

"Her husband, Robert, or Bob, as he is commonly called despite his sixty years, is quite a character in his way. He is an amusing old gossip, with a turn for racy comment and a finger in everybody's pie. He knows everything about everybody in Lindsay for three generations back.

"They have no living children, but Old Bob has a black cat which is his especial pride and darling. The name of this animal is Timothy and as such he must always be called and referred to. Never, as you value Robert's good opinion, let him hear you speaking of his pet as 'the cat,' or even as 'Tim.' You will never be forgiven and he will not consider you a fit person to have charge of the school.

"You shall have my room, a little place over the kitchen, with a ceiling that follows the slant of the roof down one side, against which you will bump your head times innumerable until you learn to remember that it is there, and a looking glass which will make one of your eyes as small as a pea and the other as big as an orange.

"But to compensate for these disadvantages the supply of towels is generous and unexceptionable; and there is a window whence you will daily behold an occidental view over Lindsay Harbour and the gulf beyond which is an unspeakable miracle of beauty. The sun is setting over it as I write and I see such a sea of glass mingled with fire as might have figured in the visions of the Patmian seer. A vessel is sailing away into the gold and crimson and pearl of the horizon; the big revolving light on the tip of the headland beyond the harbour has just been lighted and is winking and flashing like a beacon,

"'O'er the foam
  Of perilous seas in faerie lands forlorn.'"

"Wire me if you can come; and if you can, report for duty on the twenty-third of May."

Mr. Marshall, Senior, came in, just as Eric was thoughtfully folding up his letter. The former looked more like a benevolent old clergyman or philanthropist than the keen, shrewd, somewhat hard, although just and honest, man of business that he really was. He had a round, rosy face, fringed with white whiskers, a fine head of long white hair, and a pursed-up mouth. Only in his blue eyes was a twinkle that would have made any man who designed getting the better of him in a bargain think twice before he made the attempt.

It was easily seen that Eric must have inherited his personal beauty and distinction of form from his mother, whose picture hung on the dark wall between the windows. She had died while still young, when Eric was a boy of ten. During her lifetime she had been the object of the passionate devotion of both her husband and son; and the fine, strong, sweet face of the picture was a testimony that she had been worthy of their love and reverence. The same face, cast in a masculine mold, was repeated in Eric; the chestnut hair grew off his forehead in the same way; his eyes were like hers, and in his grave moods they held a similar expression, half brooding, half tender, in their depths.

Mr. Marshall was very proud of his son's success in college, but he had no intention of letting him see it. He loved this boy of his, with the dead mother's eyes, better than anything on earth, and all his hopes and ambitions were bound up in him.

"Well, that fuss is over, thank goodness," he said testily, as he dropped into his favourite chair.

"Didn't you find the programme interesting?" asked Eric absently.

"Most of it was tommyrot," said his father. "The only things I liked were Charlie's Latin prayer and those pretty little girls trotting up to get their diplomas. Latin IS the language for praying in, I do believe,—at least, when a man has a voice like Old Charlie's. There was such a sonorous roll to the words that the mere sound of them made me feel like getting down on my marrow bones. And then those girls were as pretty as pinks, now weren't they? Agnes was the finest-looking of the lot in my opinion. I hope it's true that you're courting her, Eric?"

"Confound it, father," said Eric, half irritably, half laughingly, "have you and David Baker entered into a conspiracy to hound me into matrimony whether I will or no?"

"I've never said a word to David Baker on such a subject," protested Mr. Marshall.

"Well, you are just as bad as he is. He hectored me all the way home from the college on the subject. But why are you in such a hurry to have me married, dad?"

"Because I want a homemaker in this house as soon as may be. There has never been one since your mother died. I am tired of housekeepers. And I want to see your children at my knees before I die, Eric, and I'm an old man now."

"Well, your wish is natural, father," said Eric gently, with a glance at his mother's picture. "But I can't rush out and marry somebody off-hand, can I? And I fear it wouldn't exactly do to advertise for a wife, even in these days of commercial enterprise."

"Isn't there ANYBODY you're fond of?" queried Mr. Marshall, with the patient air of a man who overlooks the frivolous jests of youth.

"No. I never yet saw the woman who could make my heart beat any faster."

"I don't know what you young men are made of nowadays," growled his father. "I was in love half a dozen times before I was your age."

"You might have been 'in love.' But you never LOVED any woman until you met my mother. I know that, father. And it didn't happen till you were pretty well on in life either."

"You're too hard to please. That's what's the matter, that's what's the matter!"

"Perhaps I am. When a man has had a mother like mine his standard of womanly sweetness is apt to be pitched pretty high. Let's drop the subject, father. Here, I want you to read this letter—it's from Larry."

"Humph!" grunted Mr. Marshall, when he had finished with it. "So Larry's knocked out at last—always thought he would be—always expected it. Sorry, too. He was a decent fellow. Well, are you going?"

"Yes, I think so, if you don't object."

"You'll have a pretty monotonous time of it, judging from his account of Lindsay."

"Probably. But I am not going over in search of excitement. I'm going to oblige Larry and have a look at the Island."

"Well, it's worth looking at, some parts of the year," conceded Mr. Marshall. "When I'm on Prince Edward Island in the summer I always understand an old Scotch Islander I met once in Winnipeg. He was always talking of 'the Island.' Somebody once asked him, 'What island do you mean?' He simply LOOKED at that ignorant man. Then he said, 'Why, Prince Edward Island, mon. WHAT OTHER ISLAND IS THERE?' Go if you'd like to. You need a rest after the grind of examinations before settling down to business. And mind you don't get into any mischief, young sir."

"Not much likelihood of that in a place like Lindsay, I fancy," laughed Eric.

"Probably the devil finds as much mischief for idle hands in Lindsay as anywhere else. The worst tragedy I ever heard of happened on a backwoods farm, fifteen miles from a railroad and five from a store. However, I expect your mother's son to behave himself in the fear of God and man. In all likelihood the worst thing that will happen to you over there will be that some misguided woman will put you to sleep in a spare room bed. And if that does happen may the Lord have mercy on your soul!"

THE MASTER OF LINDSAY SCHOOL

One evening, a month later, Eric Marshall came out of the old, white-washed schoolhouse at Lindsay, and locked the door—which was carved over with initials innumerable, and built of double plank in order that it might withstand all the assaults and batteries to which it might be subjected. Eric's pupils had gone home an hour before, but he had stayed to solve some algebra problems, and correct some Latin exercises for his advanced students.

The sun was slanting in warm yellow lines through the thick grove of maples to the west of the building, and the dim green air beneath them burst into golden bloom. A couple of sheep were nibbling the lush grass in a far corner of the play-ground; a cow-bell, somewhere in the maple woods, tinkled faintly and musically, on the still crystal air, which, in spite of its blandness, still retained a touch of the wholesome austerity and poignancy of a Canadian spring. The whole world seemed to have fallen, for the time being, into a pleasant untroubled dream.

The scene was very peaceful and pastoral—almost too much so, the young man thought, with a shrug of his shoulders, as he stood in the worn steps and gazed about him. How was he going to put in a whole month here, he wondered, with a little smile at his own expense.

"Father would chuckle if he knew I was sick of it already," he thought, as he walked across the play-ground to the long red road that ran past the school. "Well, one week is ended, at any rate. I've earned my own living for five whole days, and that is something I could never say before in all my twenty-four years of existence. It is an exhilarating thought. But teaching the Lindsay district school is distinctly NOT exhilarating—at least in such a well-behaved school as this, where the pupils are so painfully good that I haven't even the traditional excitement of thrashing obstreperous bad boys.

Everything seems to go by clock work in Lindsay educational institution. Larry must certainly have possessed a marked gift for organizing and drilling. I feel as if I were merely a big cog in an orderly machine that ran itself. However, I understand that there are some pupils who haven't shown up yet, and who, according to all reports, have not yet had the old Adam totally drilled out of them. They may make things more interesting. Also a few more compositions, such as John Reid's, would furnish some spice to professional life."

Eric's laughter wakened the echoes as he swung into the road down the long sloping hill. He had given his fourth grade pupils their own choice of subjects in the composition class that morning, and John Reid, a sober, matter-of-fact little urchin, with not the slightest embryonic development of a sense of humour, had, acting upon the whispered suggestion of a roguish desk-mate, elected to write upon "Courting." His opening sentence made Eric's face twitch mutinously whenever he recalled it during the day. "Courting is a very pleasant thing which a great many people go too far with."

The distant hills and wooded uplands were tremulous and aerial in delicate spring-time gauzes of pearl and purple. The young, green-leafed maples crowded thickly to the very edge of the road on either side, but beyond them were emerald fields basking in sunshine, over which cloud shadows rolled, broadened, and vanished. Far below the fields a calm ocean slept bluely, and sighed in its sleep, with the murmur that rings for ever in the ear of those whose good fortune it is to have been born within the sound of it.

Now and then Eric met some callow, check-shirted, bare-legged lad on horseback, or a shrewd-faced farmer in a cart, who nodded and called out cheerily, "Howdy, Master?" A young girl, with a rosy, oval face, dimpled cheeks, and pretty dark eyes filled with shy coquetry, passed him, looking as if she would not be at all averse to a better acquaintance with the new teacher.

Half way down the hill Eric met a shambling, old gray horse drawing an express wagon which had seen better days. The driver was a woman: she appeared to be one of those drab-tinted individuals who can never have felt a rosy emotion in all their lives. She stopped her horse, and beckoned Eric over to her with the knobby handle of a faded and bony umbrella.

"Reckon you're the new Master, ain't you?" she asked.

Eric admitted that he was.

"Well, I'm glad to see you," she said, offering him a hand in a much darned cotton glove that had once been black.

"I was right sorry to see Mr. West go, for he was a right good teacher, and as harmless, inoffensive a creetur as ever lived. But I always told him every time I laid eyes on him that he was in consumption, if ever a man was. YOU look real healthy—though you can't aways tell by looks, either. I had a brother complected like you, but he was killed in a railroad accident out west when he was real young.

"I've got a boy I'll be sending to school to you next week. He'd oughter gone this week, but I had to keep him home to help me put the pertaters in; for his father won't work and doesn't work and can't be made to work.

"Sandy—his full name is Edward Alexander—called after both his grandfathers—hates the idee of going to school worse 'n pisen—always did. But go he shall, for I'm determined he's got to have more larning hammered into his head yet. I reckon you'll have trouble with him, Master, for he's as stupid as an owl, and as stubborn as Solomon's mule. But mind this, Master, I'll back you up. You just lick Sandy good and plenty when he needs it, and send me a scrape of the pen home with him, and I'll give him another dose.

"There's people that always sides in with their young ones when there's any rumpus kicked up in the school, but I don't hold to that, and never did. You can depend on Rebecca Reid every time, Master."

"Thank you. I am sure I can," said Eric, in his most winning tones.

He kept his face straight until it was safe to relax, and Mrs. Reid drove on with a soft feeling in her leathery old heart, which had been so toughened by long endurance of poverty and toil, and a husband who wouldn't work and couldn't be made to work, that it was no longer a very susceptible organ where members of the opposite sex were concerned.

Mrs. Reid reflected that this young man had a way with him.

Eric already knew most of the Lindsay folks by sight; but at the foot of the hill he met two people, a man and a boy, whom he did not know. They were sitting in a shabby, old-fashioned wagon, and were watering their horse at the brook, which gurgled limpidly under the little plank bridge in the hollow.

Eric surveyed them with some curiosity. They did not look in the least like the ordinary run of Lindsay people. The boy, in particular, had a distinctly foreign appearance, in spite of the gingham shirt and homespun trousers, which seemed to be the regulation, work-a-day outfit for the Lindsay farmer lads. He had a lithe, supple body, with sloping shoulders, and a lean, satiny brown throat above his open shirt collar. His head was covered with thick, silky, black curls, and the hand that hung down by the side of the wagon was unusually long and slender. His face was richly, though somewhat heavily featured, olive tinted, save for the cheeks, which had a dusky crimson bloom. His mouth was as red and beguiling as a girl's, and his eyes were large, bold and black. All in all, he was a strikingly handsome fellow; but the expression of his face was sullen, and he somehow gave Eric the impression of a sinuous, feline creature basking in lazy grace, but ever ready for an unexpected spring.

The other occupant of the wagon was a man between sixty-five and seventy, with iron-gray hair, a long, full, gray beard, a harsh-featured face, and deep-set hazel eyes under bushy, bristling brows. He was evidently tall, with a spare, ungainly figure, and stooping shoulders. His mouth was close-lipped and relentless, and did not look as if it had ever smiled. Indeed, the idea of smiling could not be connected with this man—it was utterly incongruous. Yet there was nothing repellent about his face; and there was something in it that compelled Eric's attention.

He rather prided himself on being a student of physiognomy, and he felt quite sure that this man was no ordinary Lindsay farmer of the genial, garrulous type with which he was familiar.

Long after the old wagon, with its oddly assorted pair, had gone lumbering up the hill, Eric found himself thinking of the stern, heavy browed man and the black-eyed, red-lipped boy.

A TEA TABLE CONVERSATION

The Williamson place, where Eric boarded, was on the crest of the succeeding hill. He liked it as well as Larry West had prophesied that he would. The Williamsons, as well as the rest of the Lindsay people, took it for granted that he was a poor college student working his way through as Larry West had been doing. Eric did not disturb this belief, although he said nothing to contribute to it.

The Williamsons were at tea in the kitchen when Eric went in. Mrs. Williamson was the "saint in spectacles and calico" which Larry West had termed her. Eric liked her greatly. She was a slight, gray-haired woman, with a thin, sweet, high-bred face, deeply lined with the records of outlived pain. She talked little as a rule; but, in the pungent country phrase she never spoke but she said something. The one thing that constantly puzzled Eric was how such a woman ever came to marry Robert Williamson.

She smiled in a motherly fashion at Eric, as he hung his hat on the white-washed wall and took his place at the table. Outside of the window behind him was a birch grove which, in the westering sun, was a tremulous splendour, with a sea of undergrowth wavered into golden billows by every passing wind.

Old Robert Williamson sat opposite him, on a bench. He was a small, lean old man, half lost in loose clothes that seemed far too large for him. When he spoke his voice was as thin and squeaky as he appeared to be himself.

The other end of the bench was occupied by Timothy, sleek and complacent, with a snowy breast and white paws. After old Robert had taken a mouthful of anything he gave a piece to Timothy, who ate it daintily and purred resonant gratitude.

"You see we're busy waiting for you, Master," said old Robert. "You're late this evening. Keep any of the youngsters in? That's a foolish way of punishing them, as hard on yourself as on them. One teacher we had four years ago used to lock them in and go home. Then he'd go back in an hour and let them out—if they were there. They weren't always. Tom Ferguson kicked the panels out of the old door once and got out that way. We put a new door of double plank in that they couldn't kick out."

"I stayed in the schoolroom to do some work," said Eric briefly.

"Well, you've missed Alexander Tracy. He was here to find out if you could play checkers, and, when I told him you could, he left word for you to go up and have a game some evening soon. Don't beat him too often, even if you can. You'll need to stand in with him, I tell you, Master, for he's got a son that may brew trouble for you when he starts in to go to school. Seth Tracy's a young imp, and he'd far sooner be in mischief than eat. He tries to run on every new teacher and he's run two clean out of the school. But he met his match in Mr. West. William Tracy's boys now—you won't have a scrap of bother with THEM. They're always good because their mother tells them every Sunday that they'll go straight to hell if they don't behave in school. It's effective. Take some preserve, Master. You know we don't help things here the way Mrs. Adam Scott does when she has boarders, 'I s'pose you don't want any of this—nor you—nor you?' Mother, Aleck says old George Wright is having the time of his life. His wife has gone to Charlottetown to visit her sister and he is his own boss for the first time since he was married, forty years ago. He's on a regular orgy, Aleck says. He smokes in the parlour and sits up till eleven o'clock reading dime novels."

"Perhaps I met Mr. Tracy," said Eric. "Is he a tall man, with gray hair and a dark, stern face?"

"No, he's a round, jolly fellow, is Aleck, and he stopped growing pretty much before he'd ever begun. I reckon the man you mean is Thomas Gordon. I seen him driving down the road too. HE won't be troubling you with invitations up, small fear of it. The Gordons ain't sociable, to say the least of it. No, sir! Mother, pass the biscuits to the Master."

"Who was the young fellow he had with him?" asked Eric curiously.

"Neil—Neil Gordon."

"That is a Scotchy name for such a face and eyes. I should rather have expected Guiseppe or Angelo. The boy looks like an Italian."

"Well, now, you know, Master, I reckon it's likely he does, seeing that that's exactly what he is. You've hit the nail square on the head. Italyun, yes, sir! Rather too much so, I'm thinking, for decent folks' taste."

"How has it happened that an Italian boy with a Scotch name is living in a place like Lindsay?"

"Well, Master, it was this way. About twenty-two years ago—WAS it twenty-two, Mother or twenty-four? Yes, it was twenty-two—'twas the same year our Jim was born and he'd have been twenty-two if he'd lived, poor little fellow. Well, Master, twenty-two years ago a couple of Italian pack peddlers came along and called at the Gordon place. The country was swarming with them then. I useter set the dog on one every day on an average.

"Well, these peddlers were man and wife, and the woman took sick up there at the Gordon place, and Janet Gordon took her in and nursed her. A baby was born the next day, and the woman died. Then the first thing anybody knew the father skipped clean out, pack and all, and was never seen or heard tell of afterwards. The Gordons were left with the fine youngster to their hands. Folks advised them to send him to the Orphan Asylum, and 'twould have been the wisest plan, but the Gordons were never fond of taking advice. Old James Gordon was living then, Thomas and Janet's father, and he said he would never turn a child out of his door. He was a masterful old man and liked to be boss. Folks used to say he had a grudge against the sun 'cause it rose and set without his say so. Anyhow, they kept the baby. They called him Neil and had him baptized same as any Christian child. He's always lived there. They did well enough by him. He was sent to school and taken to church and treated like one of themselves. Some folks think they made too much of him. It doesn't always do with that kind, for 'what's bred in bone is mighty apt to come out in flesh,' if 'taint kept down pretty well. Neil's smart and a great worker, they tell me. But folks hereabouts don't like him. They say he ain't to be trusted further'n you can see him, if as far. It's certain he's awful hot tempered, and one time when he was going to school he near about killed a boy he'd took a spite to—choked him till he was black in the face and Neil had to be dragged off."

"Well now, father, you know they teased him terrible," protested Mrs. Williamson. "The poor boy had a real hard time when he went to school, Master. The other children were always casting things up to him and calling him names."

"Oh, I daresay they tormented him a lot," admitted her husband. "He's a great hand at the fiddle and likes company. He goes to the harbour a good deal. But they say he takes sulky spells when he hasn't a word to throw to a dog. 'Twouldn't be any wonder, living with the Gordons. They're all as queer as Dick's hat-band."

"Father, you shouldn't talk so about your neighbours," said his wife rebukingly.

"Well now, Mother, you know they are, if you'd only speak up honest. But you're like old Aunt Nancy Scott, you never say anything uncharitable except in the way of business. You know the Gordons ain't like other people and never were and never will be. They're about the only queer folks we have in Lindsay, Master, except old Peter Cook, who keeps twenty-five cats. Lord, Master, think of it! What chanct would a poor mouse have? None of the rest of us are queer, leastwise, we hain't found it out if we are. But, then, we're mighty uninteresting, I'm bound to admit that."

"Where do the Gordons live?" asked Eric, who had grown used to holding fast to a given point of inquiry through all the bewildering mazes of old Robert's conversation.

"Away up yander, half a mile in from Radnor road, with a thick spruce wood atween them and all the rest of the world. They never go away anywheres, except to church—they never miss that—and nobody goes there. There's just old Thomas, and his sister Janet, and a niece of theirs, and this here Neil we've been talking about. They're a queer, dour, cranky lot, and I WILL say it, Mother. There, give your old man a cup of tea and never mind the way his tongue runs on. Speaking of tea, do you know Mrs. Adam Palmer and Mrs. Jim Martin took tea together at Foster Reid's last Wednesday afternoon?"

"No, why, I thought they were on bad terms," said Mrs. Williamson, betraying a little feminine curiosity.

"So they are, so they are. But they both happened to visit Mrs. Foster the same afternoon and neither would leave because that would be knuckling down to the other. So they stuck it out, on opposite sides of the parlour. Mrs. Foster says she never spent such an uncomfortable afternoon in all her life before. She would talk a spell to one and then t'other. And they kept talking TO Mrs. Foster and AT each other. Mrs. Foster says she really thought she'd have to keep them all night, for neither would start to go home afore the other. Finally Jim Martin came in to look for his wife, 'cause he thought she must have got stuck in the marsh, and that solved the problem. Master, you ain't eating anything. Don't mind my stopping; I was at it half an hour afore you come, and anyway I'm in a hurry. My hired boy went home to-day. He heard the rooster crow at twelve last night and he's gone home to see which of his family is dead. He knows one of 'em is. He heard a rooster crow in the middle of the night onct afore and the next day he got word that his second cousin down at Souris was dead. Mother, if the Master don't want any more tea, ain't there some cream for Timothy?"

A PHANTOM OF DELIGHT

Shortly before sunset that evening Eric went for a walk. When he did not go to the shore he liked to indulge in long tramps through the Lindsay fields and woods, in the mellowness of "the sweet 'o the year." Most of the Lindsay houses were built along the main road, which ran parallel to the shore, or about the stores at "The Corner." The farms ran back from them into solitudes of woods and pasture lands.

Eric struck southwest from the Williamson homestead, in a direction he had not hitherto explored, and walked briskly along, enjoying the witchery of the season all about him in earth and air and sky. He felt it and loved it and yielded to it, as anyone of clean life and sane pulses must do.

The spruce wood in which he presently found himself was smitten through with arrows of ruby light from the setting sun. He went through it, walking up a long, purple aisle where the wood-floor was brown and elastic under his feet, and came out beyond it on a scene which surprised him.

No house was in sight, but he found himself looking into an orchard; an old orchard, evidently long neglected and forsaken. But an orchard dies hard; and this one, which must have been a very delightful spot once, was delightful still, none the less so for the air of gentle melancholy which seemed to pervade it, the melancholy which invests all places that have once been the scenes of joy and pleasure and young life, and are so no longer, places where hearts have throbbed, and pulses thrilled, and eyes brightened, and merry voices echoed. The ghosts of these things seem to linger in their old haunts through many empty years.

The orchard was large and long, enclosed in a tumbledown old fence of longers bleached to a silvery gray in the suns of many lost summers. At regular intervals along the fence were tall, gnarled fir trees, and an evening wind, sweeter than that which blew over the beds of spice from Lebanon,

27

was singing in their tops, an earth-old song with power to carry the soul back to the dawn of time.

Eastward, a thick fir wood grew, beginning with tiny treelets just feathering from the grass, and grading up therefrom to the tall veterans of the mid-grove, unbrokenly and evenly, giving the effect of a solid, sloping green wall, so beautifully compact that it looked as if it had been clipped into its velvet surface by art.

Most of the orchard was grown over lushly with grass; but at the end where Eric stood there was a square, treeless place which had evidently once served as a homestead garden. Old paths were still visible, bordered by stones and large pebbles. There were two clumps of lilac trees; one blossoming in royal purple, the other in white. Between them was a bed ablow with the starry spikes of June lilies. Their penetrating, haunting fragrance distilled on the dewy air in every soft puff of wind. Along the fence rosebushes grew, but it was as yet too early in the season for roses.

Beyond was the orchard proper, three long rows of trees with green avenues between, each tree standing in a wonderful blow of pink and white. The charm of the place took sudden possession of Eric as nothing had ever done before. He was not given to romantic fancies; but the orchard laid hold of him subtly and drew him to itself, and he was never to be quite his own man again. He went into it over one of the broken panels of fence, and so, unknowing, went forward to meet all that life held for him.

He walked the length of the orchard's middle avenue between long, sinuous boughs picked out with delicate, rose-hearted bloom. When he reached its southern boundary he flung himself down in a grassy corner of the fence where another lilac bush grew, with ferns and wild blue violets at its roots. From where he now was he got a glimpse of a house about a quarter of a mile away, its gray gable peering out from a dark spruce wood. It seemed a dull, gloomy, remote place, and he did not know who lived there.

He had a wide outlook to the west, over far hazy fields and misty blue intervales. The sun had just set, and the whole world of green meadows beyond swam in golden light. Across a long valley brimmed with shadow were uplands of sunset, and great sky lakes of saffron and rose where a soul might lose itself in colour. The air was very fragrant with the baptism of the dew, and the odours of a bed of wild mint upon which he had trampled. Robins were whistling, clear and sweet and sudden, in the woods all about him.

"This is a veritable 'haunt of ancient peace,'" quoted Eric, looking around with delighted eyes. "I could fall asleep here, dream dreams and see visions. What a sky! Could anything be diviner than that fine crystal eastern blue, and those frail white clouds that look like woven lace? What a dizzying, intoxicating fragrance lilacs have! I wonder if perfume could set a man drunk. Those apple trees now—why, what is that?"

Eric started up and listened. Across the mellow stillness, mingled with the croon of the wind in the trees and the flute-like calls of the robins, came a strain of delicious music, so beautiful and fantastic that Eric held his breath in astonishment and delight. Was he dreaming? No, it was real music, the music of a violin played by some hand inspired with the very spirit of harmony. He had never heard anything like it; and, somehow, he felt quite sure that nothing exactly like it ever had been heard before; he believed that that wonderful music was coming straight from the soul of the unseen violinist, and translating itself into those most airy and delicate and exquisite sounds for the first time; the very soul of music, with all sense and earthliness refined away.

It was an elusive, haunting melody, strangely suited to the time and place; it had in it the sigh of the wind in the woods, the eerie whispering of the grasses at dewfall, the white thoughts of the June lilies, the rejoicing of the apple blossoms; all the soul of all the old laughter and song and tears and gladness and sobs the orchard had ever known in the lost years; and besides all this, there was in it a pitiful, plaintive cry as of some imprisoned thing calling for freedom and utterance.

At first Eric listened as a man spellbound, mutely and motionlessly, lost in wonderment. Then a very natural curiosity overcame him. Who in Lindsay could play a violin like that? And who was playing so here, in this deserted old orchard, of all places in the world?

He rose and walked up the long white avenue, going as slowly and silently as possible, for he did not wish to interrupt the player. When he reached the open space of the garden he stopped short in new amazement and was again tempted into thinking he must certainly be dreaming.

Under the big branching white lilac tree was an old, sagging, wooden bench; and on this bench a girl was sitting, playing on an old brown violin. Her eyes were on the faraway horizon and she did not see Eric. For a few moments he stood there and looked at her. The pictures she made photographed itself on his vision to the finest detail, never to be blotted from his book of remembrance. To his latest day Eric Marshall will be able to recall vividly that scene as he saw it then—the velvet darkness of the spruce woods, the overarching sky of soft brilliance, the swaying lilac blossoms, and amid it all the girl on the old bench with the violin under her chin.

He had, in his twenty-four years of life, met hundreds of pretty women, scores of handsome women, a scant half dozen of really beautiful women. But he knew at once, beyond all possibility of question or doubt, that he had never seen or imagined anything so exquisite as this girl of the orchard. Her loveliness was so perfect that his breath almost went from him in his first delight of it.

Her face was oval, marked in every cameo-like line and feature with that expression of absolute, flawless purity, found in the angels and Madonnas of old paintings, a purity that held in it no faintest strain of earthliness. Her head was bare, and her thick, jet-black hair was parted above her forehead and hung in two heavy lustrous braids over her shoulders. Her eyes were of such a blue as Eric had never seen in eyes before, the tint of the sea in the still, calm light that follows after a fine sunset; they were as luminous as the stars that came out over Lindsay Harbour in the afterglow, and were fringed about with very long, soot-black lashes, and arched over by most delicately pencilled dark eyebrows. Her skin was as fine and purely tinted as the heart of a white rose. The collarless dress of pale blue print she wore revealed her smooth, slender throat; her sleeves were rolled up above her elbows and the hand which guided the bow of her violin was perhaps the most beautiful thing about her, perfect in shape and texture, firm and white, with rosy-nailed taper fingers. One long, drooping plume of lilac blossom lightly touched her hair and cast a wavering shadow over the flower-like face beneath it.

There was something very child-like about her, and yet at least eighteen sweet years must have gone to the making of her. She seemed to be playing half unconsciously, as if her thoughts were far away in some fair dreamland of the skies. But presently she looked away from "the bourne of sunset," and her lovely eyes fell on Eric, standing motionless before her in the shadow of the apple tree.

The sudden change that swept over her was startling. She sprang to her feet, the music breaking in mid-strain and the bow slipping from her hand to the grass. Every hint of colour fled from her face and she trembled like one of the wind-stirred June lilies.

"I beg your pardon," said Eric hastily. "I am sorry that I have alarmed you. But your music was so beautiful that I did not remember you were not aware of my presence here. Please forgive me."

He stopped in dismay, for he suddenly realized that the expression on the girl's face was one of terror—not merely the startled alarm of a shy, childlike creature who had thought herself alone, but absolute terror. It was betrayed in her blanched and quivering lips and in the widely distended blue eyes that stared back into his with the expression of some trapped wild thing.

It hurt him that any woman should look at him in such a fashion, at him who had always held womanhood in such reverence.

"Don't look so frightened," he said gently, thinking only of calming her fear, and speaking as he would to a child. "I will not hurt you. You are safe, quite safe."

In his eagerness to reassure her he took an unconscious step forward. Instantly she turned, and, without a sound, fled across the orchard, through a gap in the northern fence and along what seemed to be a lane bordering the fir wood beyond and arched over with wild cherry trees misty white in the gathering gloom. Before Eric could recover his wits she had vanished from his sight among the firs.

He stooped and picked up the violin bow, feeling slightly foolish and very much annoyed.

"Well, this is a most mysterious thing," he said, somewhat impatiently. "Am I bewitched? Who was she? WHAT was she? Can it be possible that she is a Lindsay girl? And why in the name of all that's provoking should she be so frightened at the mere sight of me? I have never thought I was a particularly hideous person, but certainly this adventure has not increased my vanity to any perceptible extent. Perhaps I have wandered into an enchanted orchard, and been outwardly transformed into an ogre. Now that I have come to think of it, there is something quite uncanny about the place. Anything might happen here. It is no common orchard for the production of marketable apples, that is plain to be seen. No, it's a most unwholesome locality; and the sooner I make my escape from it the better."

He glanced about it with a whimsical smile. The light was fading rapidly and the orchard was full of soft, creeping shadows and silences. It seemed to wink sleepy eyes of impish enjoyment at his perplexity. He laid the violin bow down on the old bench.

"Well, there is no use in my following her, and I have no right to do so even if it were of use. But I certainly wish she hadn't fled in such evident terror. Eyes like hers were never meant to express anything but tenderness and trust. Why—why—WHY was she so frightened? And who—who—WHO—can she be?"

All the way home, over fields and pastures that were beginning to be moonlight silvered he pondered the mystery.

"Let me see," he reflected. "Mr. Williamson was describing the Lindsay girls for my benefit the other evening. If I remember rightly he said that there were four handsome ones in the district. What were their names? Florrie Woods, Melissa Foster—no, Melissa Palmer—Emma Scott, and Jennie May Ferguson. Can she be one of them? No, it is a flagrant waste of time and gray matter supposing it. That girl couldn't be a Florrie or a Melissa or an Emma, while Jennie May is completely out of the question. Well, there is some bewitchment in the affair. Of that I'm convinced. So I'd better forget all about it."

But Eric found that it was impossible to forget all about it. The more he tried to forget, the more keenly and insistently he remembered. The girl's exquisite face haunted him and the mystery of her tantalized him.

True, he knew that, in all likelihood, he might easily solve the problem by asking the Williamsons about her. But somehow, to his own surprise, he found that he shrank from doing this. He felt that it was impossible to ask Robert Williamson and probably have the girl's name overflowed in a stream of petty gossip concerning her and all her antecedents and collaterals to the third and fourth generation. If he had to ask any one it should be Mrs. Williamson; but he meant to find out the secret for himself if it were at all possible.

He had planned to go to the harbour the next evening. One of the lobstermen had promised to take him out cod-fishing. But instead he wandered southwest over the fields again.

He found the orchard easily—he had half expected NOT to find it. It was still the same fragrant, grassy, wind-haunted spot. But it had no occupant and the violin bow was gone from the old bench.

"Perhaps she tiptoed back here for it by the light o' the moon," thought Eric, pleasing his fancy by the vision of a lithe, girlish figure stealing with a beating heart through mingled shadow and moonshine. "I wonder if she will possibly come this evening, or if I have frightened her away for ever. I'll hide me behind this spruce copse and wait."

Eric waited until dark, but no music sounded through the orchard and no one came to it. The keenness of his disappointment surprised him, nay more, it vexed him. What nonsense to be so worked up because a little girl he had seen for five minutes failed to appear! Where was his common sense, his "gumption," as old Robert Williamson would have said? Naturally a man liked to look at a pretty face. But was that any reason why he should feel as if life were flat, stale, and unprofitable simply because he could not look at it? He called himself a fool and went home in a petulant mood. Arriving there, he plunged fiercely into solving algebraical equations and working out geometry exercises, determined to put out of his head forthwith all vain imaginings of an enchanted orchard, white in the moonshine, with lilts of elfin music echoing down its long arcades.

The next day was Sunday and Eric went to church twice. The Williamson pew was one of the side ones at the top of the church and its occupants practically faced the congregation. Eric looked at every girl and woman in the audience, but he saw nothing of the face which, setting will power and common sense flatly at defiance, haunted his memory like a star.

Thomas Gordon was there, sitting alone in his long, empty pew near the top of the building; and Neil Gordon sang in the choir which occupied the front pew of the gallery. He had a powerful and melodious, though untrained voice, which dominated the singing and took the colour out of the weaker, more commonplace tones of the other singers. He was well-dressed in a suit of dark blue serge, with a white collar and tie. But Eric idly thought it did not become him so well as the working clothes in which he had first seen him. He was too obviously dressed up, and he looked coarser and more out of harmony with his surroundings.

For two days Eric refused to let himself think of the orchard. Monday evening he went cod-fishing, and Tuesday evening he went up to play checkers with Alexander Tracy. Alexander won all the games so easily that he never had any respect for Eric Marshall again.

"Played like a feller whose thoughts were wool gathering," he complained to his wife. "He'll never make a checker player—never in this world."

THE STORY OF KILMENY

Wednesday evening Eric went to the orchard again; and again he was disappointed. He went home, determined to solve the mystery by open inquiry. Fortune favoured him, for he found Mrs. Williamson alone, sitting by the west window of her kitchen and knitting at a long gray sock. She hummed softly to herself as she knitted, and Timothy slept blackly at her feet. She looked at Eric with quiet affection in her large, candid eyes. She had liked Mr. West. But Eric had found his way into the inner chamber of her heart, by reason that his eyes were so like those of the little son she had buried in the Lindsay churchyard many years before.

"Mrs. Williamson," said Eric, with an affectation of carelessness, "I chanced on an old deserted orchard back behind the woods over there last week, a charming bit of wilderness. Do you know whose it is?"

"I suppose it must be the old Connors orchard," answered Mrs. Williamson after a moment's reflection. "I had forgotten all about it. It must be all of thirty years since Mr. and Mrs. Connors moved away. Their house and barns were burned down and they sold the land to Thomas Gordon and went to live in town. They're both dead now. Mr. Connors used to be very proud of his orchard. There weren't many orchards in Lindsay then, though almost everybody has one now."

"There was a young girl in it, playing on a violin," said Eric, annoyed to find that it cost him an effort to speak of her, and that the blood mounted to his face as he did so. "She ran away in great alarm as soon as she saw me, although I do not think I did or said anything to frighten or vex her. I have no idea who she was. Do you know?"

Mrs. Williamson did not make an immediate reply. She laid down her knitting and gazed out of the window as if pondering seriously some question in her own mind. Finally she said, with an intonation of keen

35

interest in her voice,

"I suppose it must have been Kilmeny Gordon, Master."

"Kilmeny Gordon? Do you mean the niece of Thomas Gordon of whom your husband spoke?"

"Yes."

"I can hardly believe that the girl I saw can be a member of Thomas Gordon's family."

"Well, if it wasn't Kilmeny Gordon I don't know who it could have been. There is no other house near that orchard and I've heard she plays the violin. If it was Kilmeny you've seen what very few people in Lindsay have ever seen, Master. And those few have never seen her close by. I have never laid eyes on her myself. It's no wonder she ran away, poor girl. She isn't used to seeing strangers."

"I'm rather glad if that was the sole reason of her flight," said Eric. "I admit I didn't like to see any girl so frightened of me as she appeared to be. She was as white as paper, and so terrified that she never uttered a word, but fled like a deer to cover."

"Well, she couldn't have spoken a word in any case," said Mrs. Williamson quietly. "Kilmeny Gordon is dumb."

Eric sat in dismayed silence for a moment. That beautiful creature afflicted in such a fashion—why, it was horrible! Mingled with his dismay was a strange pang of personal regret and disappointment.

"It couldn't have been Kilmeny Gordon, then," he protested at last, remembering. "The girl I saw played on the violin exquisitely. I never heard anything like it. It is impossible that a deaf mute could play like that."

"Oh, she isn't deaf, Master," responded Mrs. Williamson, looking at Eric keenly through her spectacles. She picked up her knitting and fell to work again. "That is the strange part of it, if anything about her can be stranger than another. She can hear as well as anybody and understands everything that is said to her. But she can't speak a word and never could, at least, so they say. The truth is, nobody knows much about her. Janet and Thomas never speak of her, and Neil won't either. He has been well questioned, too, you can depend on that; but he won't ever say a word about Kilmeny and he gets mad if folks persist."

"Why isn't she to be spoken of?" queried Eric impatiently. "What is the mystery about her?"

"It's a sad story, Master. I suppose the Gordons look on her existence as a sort of disgrace. For my own part, I think it's terrible, the way she's been brought up. But the Gordons are very strange people, Mr. Marshall. I kind of reproved father for saying so, you remember, but it is true. They have very strange ways. And you've really seen Kilmeny? What does she look like? I've heard that she was handsome. Is it true?"

"I thought her very beautiful," said Eric rather curtly. "But HOW has she been brought up, Mrs. Williamson? And why?"

"Well, I might as well tell you the whole story, Master. Kilmeny is the niece of Thomas and Janet Gordon. Her mother was Margaret Gordon, their younger sister. Old James Gordon came out from Scotland. Janet and Thomas were born in the Old Country and were small children when they came here. They were never very sociable folks, but still they used to visit out some then, and people used to go there. They were kind and honest people, even if they were a little peculiar.

"Mrs. Gordon died a few years after they came out, and four years later James Gordon went home to Scotland and brought a new wife back with him. She was a great deal younger than he was and a very pretty woman, as my mother often told me. She was friendly and gay and liked social life. The Gordon place was a very different sort of place after she came there, and even Janet and Thomas got thawed out and softened down a good bit. They were real fond of their stepmother, I've heard. Then, six years after she was married, the second Mrs. Gordon died too. She died when Margaret was born. They say James Gordon almost broke his heart over it.

"Janet brought Margaret up. She and Thomas just worshipped the child and so did their father. I knew Margaret Gordon well once. We were just the same age and we set together in school. We were always good friends until she turned against all the world.

"She was a strange girl in some ways even then, but I always liked her, though a great many people didn't. She had some bitter enemies, but she had some devoted friends too. That was her way. She made folks either hate or love her. Those who did love her would have gone through fire and water for her.

"When she grew up she was very pretty—tall and splendid, like a queen, with great thick braids of black hair and red, red cheeks and lips. Everybody who saw her looked at her a second time. She was a little vain of her beauty, I think, Master. And she was proud, oh, she was very proud. She liked to be first in everything, and she couldn't bear not to show to good advantage. She was dreadful determined, too. You couldn't budge her an inch, Master, when she once had made up her mind on any point. But she was warm-hearted and generous. She could sing like an angel and she was very clever. She could learn anything with just one look at it and she was terrible fond of reading.

"When I'm talking about her like this it all comes back to me, just what she was like and how she looked and spoke and acted, and little ways she had of moving her hands and head. I declare it almost seems as if she was right here in this room instead of being over there in the churchyard. I wish you'd light the lamp, Master. I feel kind of nervous."

Eric rose and lighted the lamp, rather wondering at Mrs. Williamson's unusual exhibition of nerves. She was generally so calm and composed.

"Thank you, Master. That's better. I won't be fancying now that Margaret Gordon's here listening to what I'm saying. I had the feeling so strong a moment ago.

"I suppose you think I'm a long while getting to Kilmeny, but I'm coming to that. I didn't mean to talk so much about Margaret, but somehow my thoughts got taken up with her.

"Well, Margaret passed the Board and went to Queen's Academy and got a teacher's license. She passed pretty well up when she came out, but Janet told me she cried all night after the pass list came out because there were some ahead of her.

"She went to teach school over at Radnor. It was there she met a man named Ronald Fraser. Margaret had never had a beau before. She could have had any young man in Lindsay if she had wanted him, but she wouldn't look at one of them. They said it was because she thought nobody was good enough for her, but that wasn't the way of it at all, Master. I knew, because Margaret and I used to talk of those matters, as girls do. She didn't believe in going with anybody unless it was somebody she thought everything of. And there was nobody in Lindsay she cared that much for.

"This Ronald Fraser was a stranger from Nova Scotia and nobody knew much about him. He was a widower, although he was only a young man. He had set up store-keeping in Radnor and was doing well. He was real handsome and had taking ways women like. It was said that all the Radnor girls were in love with him, but I don't think his worst enemy could have said he flirted with them. He never took any notice of them; but the very first time he saw Margaret Gordon he fell in love with her and she with him.

"They came over to church in Lindsay together the next Sunday and everybody said it would be a match. Margaret looked lovely that day, so gentle and womanly. She had been used to hold her head pretty high, but that day she held it drooping a little and her black eyes cast down. Ronald Fraser was very tall and fair, with blue eyes. They made as handsome a couple as I ever saw.

"But old James Gordon and Thomas and Janet didn't much approve of him. I saw that plain enough one time I was there and he brought Margaret home from Radnor Friday night. I guess they wouldn't have liked anybody, though, who come after Margaret. They thought nobody was good enough for her.

"But Margaret coaxed them all round in time. She could do pretty near anything with them, they were so fond and proud of her. Her father held out the longest, but finally he give in and consented for her to marry Ronald Fraser.

"They had a big wedding, too—all the neighbours were asked. Margaret always liked to make a display. I was her bridesmaid, Master. I helped her dress and nothing would please her; she wanted to look that nice for Ronald's sake. She was a handsome bride; dressed in white, with red roses in her hair and at her breast. She wouldn't wear white flowers; she said they looked too much like funeral flowers. She looked like a picture. I can see her this minute, as plain as plain, just as she was that night, blushing and turning pale by turns, and looking at Ronald with her eyes of love. If ever a girl loved a man with all her heart Margaret Gordon did. It almost made me feel frightened. She gave him the worship it isn't right to give anybody but God, Master, and I think that is always punished.

"They went to live at Radnor and for a little while everything went well. Margaret had a nice house, and was gay and happy. She dressed beautiful and entertained a good deal. Then—well, Ronald Fraser's first wife turned up looking for him! She wasn't dead after all.

"Oh, there was terrible scandal, Master. The talk and gossip was something dreadful. Every one you met had a different story, and it was hard to get at the truth. Some said Ronald Fraser had known all the time that his wife wasn't dead, and had deceived Margaret. But I don't think he did. He swore he didn't. They hadn't been very happy together, it seems. Her mother made trouble between them. Then she went to visit her mother in Montreal, and died in the hospital there, so the word came to Ronald. Perhaps he believed it a little too readily, but that he DID believe it I never had a doubt. Her story was that it was another woman of the same name. When she found out Ronald thought her dead she and her mother agreed to let him think so. But when she heard he had got married again she thought she'd better let him know the truth.

"It all sounded like a queer story and I suppose you couldn't blame people for not believing it too readily. But I've always felt it was true. Margaret didn't think so, though. She believed that Ronald Fraser had deceived her, knowing all the time that he couldn't make her his lawful wife. She turned against him and hated him just as much as she had loved him before.

"Ronald Fraser went away with his real wife, and in less than a year word came of his death. They said he just died of a broken heart, nothing more nor less.

"Margaret came home to her father's house. From the day that she went over its threshold, she never came out until she was carried out in her coffin three years ago. Not a soul outside of her own family ever saw her again. I went to see her, but Janet told me she wouldn't see me. It was foolish of Margaret to act so. She hadn't done anything real wrong; and everybody was sorry for her and would have helped her all they could. But I reckon pity cut her as deep as blame could have done, and deeper, because you see, Master, she was so proud she couldn't bear it.

"They say her father was hard on her, too; and that was unjust if it was true. Janet and Thomas felt the disgrace, too. The people that had been in the habit of going to the Gordon place soon stopped going, for they could see they were not welcome.

"Old James Gordon died that winter. He never held his head up again after the scandal. He had been an elder in the church, but he handed in his resignation right away and nobody could persuade him to withdraw it.

"Kilmeny was born in the spring, but nobody ever saw her, except the minister who baptized her. She was never taken to church or sent to school. Of course, I suppose there wouldn't have been any use in her going to school when she couldn't speak, and it's likely Margaret taught her all she could be taught herself. But it was dreadful that she was never taken to church, or let go among the children and young folks. And it was a real shame that nothing was ever done to find out why she couldn't talk, or if she could be cured.

"Margaret Gordon died three years ago, and everybody in Lindsay went to the funeral. But they didn't see her. The coffin lid was screwed down. And they didn't see Kilmeny either. I would have loved to see HER for Margaret's sake, but I didn't want to see poor Margaret. I had never seen her since the night she was a bride, for I had left Lindsay on a visit just after that, and what I came home the scandal had just broken out. I remembered Margaret in all her pride and beauty, and I couldn't have borne to look at her dead face and see the awful changes I knew must be there.

"It was thought perhaps Janet and Thomas would take Kilmeny out after her mother was gone, but they never did, so I suppose they must have agreed with Margaret about the way she had been brought up. I've often felt sorry for the poor girl, and I don't think her people did right by her, even if she was mysteriously afflicted. She must have had a very sad, lonely life.

"That is the story, Master, and I've been a long time telling it, as I dare say you think. But the past just seemed to be living again for me as I talked. If you don't want to be pestered with questions about Kilmeny Gordon, Master, you'd better not let on you've seen her."

Eric was not likely to. He had heard all he wanted to know and more.

"So this girl is at the core of a tragedy," he reflected, as he went to his room. "And she is dumb! The pity of it! Kilmeny! The name suits her. She is as lovely and innocent as the heroine of the old ballad. 'And oh, Kilmeny was fair to see.' But the next line is certainly not so appropriate, for her eyes were anything but 'still and steadfast'—after she had seen me, at all events."

He tried to put her out of his thoughts, but he could not. The memory of her beautiful face drew him with a power he could not resist. The next evening he went again to the orchard.

A ROSE OF WOMANHOOD

When he emerged from the spruce wood and entered the orchard his heart gave a sudden leap, and he felt that the blood rushed madly to his face. She was there, bending over the bed of June lilies in the centre of the garden plot. He could only see her profile, virginal and white.

He stopped, not wishing to startle her again. When she lifted her head he expected to see her shrink and flee, but she did not do so; she only grew a little paler and stood motionless, watching him intently.

Seeing this, he walked slowly towards her, and when he was so close to her that he could hear the nervous flutter of her breath over her parted, trembling lips, he said very gently,

"Do not be afraid of me. I am a friend, and I do not wish to disturb or annoy you in any way."

She seemed to hesitate a moment. Then she lifted a little slate that hung at her belt, wrote something on it rapidly, and held it out to him. He read, in a small distinctive handwriting,

"I am not afraid of you now. Mother told me that all strange men were very wicked and dangerous, but I do not think you can be. I have thought a great deal about you, and I am sorry I ran away the other night."

He realized her entire innocence and simplicity. Looking earnestly into her still troubled eyes he said,

"I would not do you any harm for the world. All men are not wicked, although it is too true that some are so. My name is Eric Marshall and I am teaching in the Lindsay school. You, I think, are Kilmeny Gordon. I thought your music so very lovely the other evening that I have been wishing ever since that I might hear it again. Won't you play for me?"

The vague fear had all gone from her eyes by this time, and suddenly she smiled—a merry, girlish, wholly irresistible smile, which broke through the

43

calm of her face like a gleam of sunlight rippling over a placid sea. Then she wrote, "I am very sorry that I cannot play this evening. I did not bring my violin with me. But I will bring it to-morrow evening and play for you if you would like to hear me. I should like to please you."

Again that note of innocent frankness! What a child she was—what a beautiful, ignorant child, utterly unskilled in the art of hiding her feelings! But why should she hide them? They were as pure and beautiful as herself. Eric smiled back at her with equal frankness.

"I should like it more than I can say, and I shall be sure to come to-morrow evening if it is fine. But if it is at all damp or unpleasant you must not come. In that case another evening will do. And now won't you give me some flowers?"

She nodded, with another little smile, and began to pick some of the June lilies, carefully selecting the most perfect among them. He watched her lithe, graceful motions with delight; every movement seemed poetry itself. She looked like a very incarnation of Spring—as if all the shimmer of young leaves and glow of young mornings and evanescent sweetness of young blossoms in a thousand springs had been embodied in her.

When she came to him, radiant, her hands full of the lilies, a couplet from a favourite poem darted into his head—

"A blossom vermeil white
That lightly breaks a faded flower sheath,
Here, by God's rood, is the one maid for me."

The next moment he was angry with himself for his folly. She was, after all, nothing but a child—and a child set apart from her fellow creatures by her sad defect. He must not let himself think nonsense.

"Thank you. These June lilies are the sweetest flowers the spring brings us. Do you know that their real name is the white narcissus?" She looked pleased and interested.

"No, I did not know," she wrote. "I have often read of the white narcissus and wondered what it was like. I never thought of it being the same as my dear June lilies. I am glad you told me. I love flowers very much. They are my very good friends."

"You couldn't help being friends with the lilies. Like always takes to like," said Eric. "Come and sit down on the old bench—here, where you were sitting that night I frightened you so badly. I could not imagine who or what you were. Sometimes I thought I had dreamed you—only," he added under his breath and unheard by her, "I could never have dreamed anything half so lovely."

She sat down beside him on the old bench and looked unshrinkingly in his face. There was no boldness in her glance—nothing but the most perfect, childlike trust and confidence. If there had been any evil in his heart—any skulking thought, he was afraid to acknowledge—those eyes must have searched it out and shamed it. But he could meet them unafraid. Then she wrote,

"I was very much frightened. You must have thought me very silly, but I had never seen any man except Uncle Thomas and Neil and the egg peddler. And you are different from them—oh, very, very different. I was afraid to come back here the next evening. And yet, somehow, I wanted to come. I did not want you to think I did not know how to behave. I sent Neil back for my bow in the morning. I could not do without it. I cannot speak, you know. Are you sorry?"

"I am very sorry for your sake."

"Yes, but what I mean is, would you like me better if I could speak like other people?"

"No, it does not make any difference in that way, Kilmeny. By the way, do you mind my calling you Kilmeny?"

She looked puzzled and wrote, "What else should you call me? That is my name. Everybody calls me that."

"But I am such a stranger to you that perhaps you would wish me to call you Miss Gordon."

"Oh, no, I would not like that," she wrote quickly, with a distressed look on her face. "Nobody ever calls me that. It would make me feel as if I were not myself but somebody else. And you do not seem like a stranger to me. Is there any reason why you should not call me Kilmeny?"

"No reason whatever, if you will allow me the privilege. You have a very lovely name—the very name you ought to have."

"I am glad you like it. Do you know that I was called after my grandmother and she was called after a girl in a poem? Aunt Janet has never liked my name, although she liked my grandmother. But I am glad you like both my name and me. I was afraid you would not like me because I cannot speak."

"You can speak through your music, Kilmeny."

She looked pleased. "How well you understand," she wrote. "Yes, I cannot speak or sing as other people can, but I can make my violin say things for me."

"Do you compose your own music?" he asked. But he saw she did not understand him. "I mean, did any one ever teach you the music you played here that evening?"

"Oh, no. It just came as I thought. It has always been that way. When I was very little Neil taught me to hold the violin and the bow, and the rest all came of itself. My violin once belonged to Neil, but he gave it to me. Neil is very good and kind to me, but I like you better. Tell me about yourself."

The wonder of her grew upon him with every passing moment. How lovely she was! What dear little ways and gestures she had—ways and gestures as artless and unstudied as they were effective. And how strangely little her dumbness seemed to matter after all! She wrote so quickly and easily, her eyes and smile gave such expression to her mobile face, that voice was hardly missed.

They lingered in the orchard until the long, languid shadows of the trees crept to their feet. It was just after sunset and the distant hills were purple against the melting saffron of the sky in the west and the crystalline blue of the sky in the south. Eastward, just over the fir woods, were clouds, white and high heaped like snow mountains, and the westernmost of them shone with a rosy glow as of sunset on an Alpine height.

The higher worlds of air were still full of light—perfect, stainless light, unmarred of earth shadow; but down in the orchard and under the spruces the light had almost gone, giving place to a green, dewy dusk, made passionately sweet with the breath of the apple blossoms and mint, and the balsamic odours that rained down upon them from the firs.

Eric told her of his life, and the life in the great outer world, in which she was girlishly and eagerly interested. She asked him many questions about it—direct and incisive questions which showed that she had already formed decided opinions and views about it. Yet it was plain to be seen that she did not regard it as anything she might ever share herself. Hers was the dispassionate interest with which she might have listened to a tale of the land of fairy or of some great empire long passed away from earth.

Eric discovered that she had read a great deal of poetry and history, and a few books of biography and travel. She did not know what a novel meant and had never heard of one. Curiously enough, she was well informed regarding politics and current events, from the weekly paper for which her uncle subscribed.

"I never read the newspaper while mother was alive," she wrote, "nor any poetry either. She taught me to read and write and I read the Bible all through many times and some of the histories. After mother died Aunt Janet gave me all her books. She had a great many. Most of them had been given to her as prizes when she was a girl at school, and some of them had been given to her by my father. Do you know the story of my father and mother?"

Eric nodded.

"Yes, Mrs. Williamson told me all about it. She was a friend of your mother."

"I am glad you have heard it. It is so sad that I would not like to tell it, but you will understand everything better because you know. I never heard it until just before mother died. Then she told me all. I think she had thought father was to blame for the trouble; but before she died she told me she believed that she had been unjust to him and that he had not known. She said that when people were dying they saw things more clearly and she saw she had made a mistake about father. She said she had many more things she wanted to tell me, but she did not have time to tell them because she died that night. It was a long while before I had the heart to read her books. But when I did I thought them so beautiful. They were poetry and it was like music put into words."

"I will bring you some books to read, if you would like them," said Eric.

Her great blue eyes gleamed with interest and delight.

"Oh, thank you, I would like it very much. I have read mine over so often that I know them nearly all by heart. One cannot get tired of really beautiful things, but sometimes I feel that I would like some new books."

"Are you never lonely, Kilmeny?"

"Oh, no, how could I be? There is always plenty for me to do, helping Aunt Janet about the house. I can do a great many things"—she glanced up at him with a pretty pride as her flying pencil traced the words. "I can cook and sew. Aunt Janet says I am a very good housekeeper, and she does not praise people very often or very much. And then, when I am not helping her, I have my dear, dear violin. That is all the company I want. But I like to read and hear of the big world so far away and the people who live there and the things that are done. It must be a very wonderful place."

"Wouldn't you like to go out into it and see its wonders and meet those people yourself?" he asked, smiling at her.

At once he saw that, in some way he could not understand, he had hurt her. She snatched her pencil and wrote, with such swiftness of motion and energy of expression that it almost seemed as if she had passionately exclaimed the words aloud,

"No, no, no. I do not want to go anywhere away from home. I do not want ever to see strangers or have them see me. I could not bear it."

He thought that possibly the consciousness of her defect accounted for this. Yet she did not seem sensitive about her dumbness and made frequent casual references to it in her written remarks. Or perhaps it was the shadow on her birth. Yet she was so innocent that it seemed unlikely she could realize or understand the existence of such a shadow. Eric finally decided that it was merely the rather morbid shrinking of a sensitive child who had been brought up in an unwholesome and unnatural way. At last the lengthening shadows warned him that it was time to go.

"You won't forget to come to-morrow evening and play for me," he said, rising reluctantly. She answered by a quick little shake of her sleek, dark head, and a smile that was eloquent. He watched her as she walked across the orchard,

"With the moon's beauty and the moon's soft pace,"

and along the wild cherry lane. At the corner of the firs she paused and waved her hand to him before turning it.

When Eric reached home old Robert Williamson was having a lunch of bread and milk in the kitchen. He looked up, with a friendly grin, as Eric strode in, whistling.

"Been having a walk, Master?" he queried.

"Yes," said Eric.

Unconsciously and involuntarily he infused so much triumph into the simple monosyllable that even old Robert felt it. Mrs. Williamson, who was cutting bread at the end of the table, laid down her knife and loaf, and looked at the young man with a softly troubled expression in her eyes. She wondered if he had been back to the Connors orchard—and if he could have seen Kilmeny Gordon again.

"You didn't discover a gold mine, I s'pose?" said old Robert dryly. "You look as if you might have."

AT THE GATE OF EDEN

When Eric went to the old Connors orchard the next evening he found
Kilmeny waiting for him on the bench under the white lilac tree, with the
violin in her lap. As soon as she saw him she caught it up and began to play
an airy delicate little melody that sounded like the laughter of daisies.

When it was finished she dropped her bow, and looked up at him with
flushed cheeks and questioning eyes.

"What did that say to you?" she wrote.

"It said something like this," answered Eric, falling into her humour
smilingly. "Welcome, my friend. It is a very beautiful evening. The sky is so
blue and the apple blossoms so sweet. The wind and I have been here alone
together and the wind is a good companion, but still I am glad to see you. It
is an evening on which it is good to be alive and to wander in an orchard
that is fine and white. Welcome, my friend."

She clapped her hands, looking like a pleased child.

"You are very quick to understand," she wrote. "That was just what I
meant. Of course I did not think it in just those words, but that was the
FEELING of it. I felt that I was so glad I was alive, and that the apple
blossoms and the white lilacs and the trees and I were all pleased together
to see you come. You are quicker than Neil. He is almost always puzzled to
understand my music, and I am puzzled to understand his. Sometimes it
frightens me. It seems as if there were something in it trying to take hold of
me—something I do not like and want to run away from."

Somehow Eric did not like her references to Neil. The idea of that
handsome, low-born boy seeing Kilmeny every day, talking to her, sitting at
the same table with her, dwelling under the same roof, meeting her in the
hundred intimacies of daily life, was distasteful to him. He put the thought
away from him, and flung himself down on the long grass at her feet.

"Now play for me, please," he said. "I want to lie here and listen to you."
"And look at you," he might have added. He could not tell which was the greater pleasure. Her beauty, more wonderful than any pictured loveliness he had ever seen, delighted him. Every tint and curve and outline of her face was flawless. Her music enthralled him. This child, he told himself as he listened, had genius. But it was being wholly wasted. He found himself thinking resentfully of the people who were her guardians, and who were responsible for her strange life. They had done her a great and irremediable wrong. How dared they doom her to such an existence? If her defect of utterance had been attended to in time, who knew but that it might have been cured? Now it was probably too late. Nature had given her a royal birthright of beauty and talent, but their selfish and unpardonable neglect had made it of no account.

What divine music she lured out of the old violin—merry and sad, gay and sorrowful by turns, music such as the stars of morning might have made singing together, music that the fairies might have danced to in their revels among the green hills or on yellow sands, music that might have mourned over the grave of a dead hope. Then she drifted into a still sweeter strain. As he listened to it he realized that the whole soul and nature of the girl were revealing themselves to him through her music—the beauty and purity of her thoughts, her childhood dreams and her maiden reveries. There was no thought of concealment about her; she could not help the revelation she was unconscious of making.

At last she laid her violin aside and wrote,

"I have done my best to give you pleasure. It is your turn now. Do you remember a promise you made me last night? Have you kept it?"

He gave her the two books he had brought for her—a modern novel and a volume of poetry unknown to her. He had hesitated a little over the former; but the book was so fine and full of beauty that he thought it could not bruise the bloom of her innocence ever so slightly. He had no doubts about the poetry. It was the utterance of one of those great inspired souls whose passing tread has made the kingdom of their birth and labour a veritable Holy Land.

He read her some of the poems. Then he talked to her of his college days and friends. The minutes passed very swiftly. There was just then no world for him outside of that old orchard with its falling blossoms and its shadows and its crooning winds.

Once, when he told her the story of some college pranks wherein the endless feuds of freshmen and sophomores figured, she clapped her hands together according to her habit, and laughed aloud—a clear, musical, silvery peal. It fell on Eric's ear with a shock of surprise. He thought it strange that she could laugh like that when she could not speak. Wherein lay the defect that closed for her the gates of speech? Was it possible that it could be removed?

"Kilmeny," he said gravely after a moment's reflection, during which he had looked up as she sat with the ruddy sunlight falling through the lilac branches on her bare, silky head like a shower of red jewels, "do you mind if I ask you something about your inability to speak? Will it hurt you to talk of the matter with me?"

She shook her head.

"Oh, no," she wrote, "I do not mind at all. Of course I am sorry I cannot speak, but I am quite used to the thought and it never hurts me at all."

"Then, Kilmeny, tell me this. Do you know why it is that you are unable to speak, when all your other faculties are so perfect?"

"No, I do not know at all why I cannot speak. I asked mother once and she told me it was a judgment on her for a great sin she had committed, and she looked so strangely that I was frightened, and I never spoke of it to her or anyone else again."

"Were you ever taken to a doctor to have your tongue and organs of speech examined?"

"No. I remember when I was a very little girl that Uncle Thomas wanted to take me to a doctor in Charlottetown and see if anything could be done for me, but mother would not let him. She said it would be no use. And I do not think Uncle Thomas thought it would be, either."

"You can laugh very naturally. Can you make any other sound?"

"Yes, sometimes. When I am pleased or frightened I have made little cries. But it is only when I am not thinking of it at all that I can do that. If I TRY to make a sound I cannot do it at all."

This seemed to Eric more mysterious than ever.

"Do you ever try to speak—to utter words?" he persisted.

"Oh yes, very often. All the time I am saying the words in my head, just as I hear other people saying them, but I never can make my tongue say them. Do not look so sorry, my friend. I am very happy and I do not mind so very much not being able to speak—only sometimes when I have so many thoughts and it seems so slow to write them out, some of them get away from me. I must play to you again. You look too sober."

She laughed again, picked up her violin, and played a tinkling, roguish little melody as if she were trying to tease him, looking at Eric over her violin with luminous eyes that dared him to be merry.

Eric smiled; but the puzzled look returned to his face many times that evening. He walked home in a brown study. Kilmeny's case certainly seemed a strange one, and the more he thought of it the stranger it seemed.

"It strikes me as something very peculiar that she should be able to make sounds only when she is not thinking about it," he reflected. "I wish David Baker could examine her. But I suppose that is out of the question. That grim pair who have charge of her would never consent."

THE STRAIGHT SIMPLICITY OF EVE

For the next three weeks Eric Marshall seemed to himself to be living two lives, as distinct from each other as if he possessed a double personality. In one, he taught the Lindsay district school diligently and painstakingly; solved problems; argued on theology with Robert Williamson; called at the homes of his pupils and took tea in state with their parents; went to a rustic dance or two and played havoc, all unwittingly, with the hearts of the Lindsay maidens.

But this life was a dream of workaday. He only LIVED in the other, which was spent in an old orchard, grassy and overgrown, where the minutes seemed to lag for sheer love of the spot and the June winds made wild harping in the old spruces.

Here every evening he met Kilmeny; in that old orchard they garnered hours of quiet happiness together; together they went wandering in the fair fields of old romance; together they read many books and talked of many things; and, when they were tired of all else, Kilmeny played to him and the old orchard echoed with her lovely, fantastic melodies.

At every meeting her beauty came home afresh to him with the old thrill of glad surprise. In the intervals of absence it seemed to him that she could not possibly be as beautiful as he remembered her; and then when they met she seemed even more so. He learned to watch for the undisguised light of welcome that always leaped into her eyes at the sound of his footsteps. She was nearly always there before him and she always showed that she was glad to see him with the frank delight of a child watching for a dear comrade.

She was never in the same mood twice. Now she was grave, now gay, now stately, now pensive. But she was always charming. Thrawn and twisted the old Gordon stock might be, but it had at least this one offshoot of perfect grace and symmetry. Her mind and heart, utterly unspoiled of the world, were as beautiful as her face. All the ugliness of existence had passed her by, shrined in her double solitude of upbringing and muteness.

She was naturally quick and clever. Delightful little flashes of wit and humour sparkled out occasionally. She could be whimsical—even charmingly capricious. Sometimes innocent mischief glimmered out in the unfathomable deeps of her blue eyes. Sarcasm, even, was not unknown to her. Now and then she punctured some harmless bubble of a young man's conceit or masculine superiority with a biting little line of daintily written script.

She assimilated the ideas in the books they read, speedily, eagerly, and thoroughly, always seizing on the best and truest, and rejecting the false and spurious and weak with an unfailing intuition at which Eric marvelled. Hers was the spear of Ithuriel, trying out the dross of everything and leaving only the pure gold.

In manner and outlook she was still a child. Yet now and again she was as old as Eve. An expression would leap into her laughing face, a subtle meaning reveal itself in her smile, that held all the lore of womanhood and all the wisdom of the ages.

Her way of smiling enchanted him. The smile always began far down in her eyes and flowed outward to her face like a sparkling brook stealing out of shadow into sunshine.

He knew everything about her life. She told him her simple history freely. She often mentioned her uncle and aunt and seemed to regard them with deep affection. She rarely spoke of her mother. Eric came somehow to understand, less from what she said than from what she did not say, that Kilmeny, though she had loved her mother, had always been rather afraid of her. There had not been between them the natural beautiful confidence of mother and child.

Of Neil, she wrote frequently at first, and seemed very fond of him. Later she ceased to mention him. Perhaps—for she was marvellously quick to catch and interpret every fleeting change of expression in his voice and face—she discerned what Eric did not know himself—that his eyes clouded and grew moody at the mention of Neil's name.

Once she asked him naively,

"Are there many people like you out in the world?"

"Thousands of them," said Eric, laughing.

She looked gravely at him. Then she gave her head a quick decided little shake.

"I do not think so," she wrote. "I do not know much of the world, but I do not think there are many people like you in it."

One evening, when the far-away hills and fields were scarfed in gauzy purples, and the intervales were brimming with golden mists, Eric carried to the old orchard a little limp, worn volume that held a love story. It was the first thing of the kind he had ever read to her, for in the first novel he had lent her the love interest had been very slight and subordinate. This was a beautiful, passionate idyl exquisitely told.

He read it to her, lying in the grass at her feet; she listened with her hands clasped over her knee and her eyes cast down. It was not a long story; and when he had finished it he shut the book and looked up at her questioningly.

"Do you like it, Kilmeny?" he asked.

Very slowly she took her slate and wrote,

"Yes, I like it. But it hurt me, too. I did not know that a person could like anything that hurt her. I do not know why it hurt me. I felt as if I had lost something that I never had. That was a very silly feeling, was it not? But I did not understand the book very well, you see. It is about love and I do not know anything about love. Mother told me once that love is a curse, and that I must pray that it would never enter into my life. She said it very earnestly, and so I believed her. But your book teaches that it is a blessing. It says that it is the most splendid and wonderful thing in life. Which am I to believe?"

"Love—real love—is never a curse, Kilmeny," said Eric gravely. "There is a false love which IS a curse. Perhaps your mother believed it was that which had entered her life and ruined it; and so she made the mistake. There is nothing in the world—or in heaven either, as I believe—so truly beautiful and wonderful and blessed as love."

"Have you ever loved?" asked Kilmeny, with the directness of phrasing necessitated by her mode of communication which was sometimes a little terrible. She asked the question simply and without embarrassment. She knew of no reason why love might not be discussed with Eric as other matters—music and books and travel—might be.

"No," said Eric—honestly, as he thought, "but every one has an ideal of love whom he hopes to meet some day—'the ideal woman of a young man's dream.' I suppose I have mine, in some sealed, secret chamber of my heart."

"I suppose your ideal woman would be beautiful, like the woman in your book?"

"Oh, yes, I am sure I could never care for an ugly woman," said Eric, laughing a little as he sat up. "Our ideals are always beautiful, whether they so translate themselves into realities or not. But the sun is going down. Time does certainly fly in this enchanted orchard. I believe you bewitch the moments away, Kilmeny. Your namesake of the poem was a somewhat uncanny maid, if I recollect aright, and thought as little of seven years in elfland as ordinary folk do of half an hour on upper earth. Some day I shall waken from a supposed hour's lingering here and find myself an old man with white hair and ragged coat, as in that fairy tale we read the other night.

Will you let me give you this book? I should never commit the sacrilege of reading it in any other place than this. It is an old book, Kilmeny. A new book, savouring of the shop and market-place, however beautiful it might be, would not do for you. This was one of my mother's books. She read it and loved it. See—the faded rose leaves she placed in it one day are there still. I'll write your name in it—that quaint, pretty name of yours which always sounds as if it had been specially invented for you—'Kilmeny of the Orchard'—and the date of this perfect June day on which we read it together. Then when you look at it you will always remember me, and the white buds opening on that rosebush beside you, and the rush and murmur of the wind in the tops of those old spruces."

He held out the book to her, but, to his surprise, she shook her head, with a deeper flush on her face.

"Won't you take the book, Kilmeny? Why not?"

She took her pencil and wrote slowly, unlike her usual quick movement.

"Do not be offended with me. I shall not need anything to make me remember you because I can never forget you. But I would rather not take the book. I do not want to read it again. It is about love, and there is no use in my learning about love, even if it is all you say. Nobody will ever love me. I am too ugly."

"You! Ugly!" exclaimed Eric. He was on the point of going off into a peal of laughter at the idea when a glimpse of her half averted face sobered him. On it was a hurt, bitter look, such as he remembered seeing once before, when he had asked her if she would not like to see the world for herself.

"Kilmeny," he said in astonishment, "you don't really think yourself ugly, do you?"

She nodded, without looking at him, and then wrote,

"Oh, yes, I know that I am. I have known it for a long time. Mother told me that I was very ugly and that nobody would ever like to look at me. I am sorry. It hurts me much worse to know I am ugly than it does to know I cannot speak. I suppose you will think that is very foolish of me, but it is true. That was why I did not come back to the orchard for such a long time, even after I had got over my fright. I hated to think that YOU would think me ugly. And that is why I do not want to go out into the world and meet people. They would look at me as the egg peddler did one day when I went out with Aunt Janet to his wagon the spring after mother died. He stared at me so. I knew it was because he thought me so ugly, and I have always hidden when he came ever since."

Eric's lips twitched. In spite of his pity for the real suffering displayed in her eyes, he could not help feeling amused over the absurd idea of this beautiful girl believing herself in all seriousness to be ugly.

"But, Kilmeny, do you think yourself ugly when you look in a mirror?" he asked smiling.

"I have never looked in a mirror," she wrote. "I never knew there was such a thing until after mother died, and I read about it in a book. Then I asked Aunt Janet and she said mother had broken all the looking glasses in the house when I was a baby. But I have seen my face reflected in the spoons, and in a little silver sugar bowl Aunt Janet has. And it IS ugly—very ugly."

Eric's face went down into the grass. For his life he could not help laughing; and for his life he would not let Kilmeny see him laughing. A certain little whimsical wish took possession of him and he did not hasten to tell her the truth, as had been his first impulse. Instead, when he dared to look up he said slowly,

"I don't think you are ugly, Kilmeny."

"Oh, but I am sure you must," she wrote protestingly. "Even Neil does. He tells me I am kind and nice, but one day I asked him if he thought me very ugly, and he looked away and would not speak, so I knew what he thought about it, too. Do not let us speak of this again. It makes me feel sorry and spoils everything. I forget it at other times. Let me play you some good-bye music, and do not feel vexed because I would not take your book. It would only make me unhappy to read it."

"I am not vexed," said Eric, "and I think you will take it some day yet—after I have shown you something I want you to see. Never mind about your looks, Kilmeny. Beauty isn't everything."

"Oh, it is a great deal," she wrote naively. "But you do like me, even though I am so ugly, don't you? You like me because of my beautiful music, don't you?"

"I like you very much, Kilmeny," answered Eric, laughing a little; but there was in his voice a tender note of which he was unconscious. Kilmeny was aware of it, however, and she picked up her violin with a pleased smile.

He left her playing there, and all the way through the dim resinous spruce wood her music followed him like an invisible guardian spirit.

"Kilmeny the Beautiful!" he murmured, "and yet, good heavens, the child thinks she is ugly—she with a face more lovely than ever an artist dreamed of! A girl of eighteen who has never looked in a mirror! I wonder if there is another such in any civilized country in the world. What could have possessed her mother to tell her such a falsehood? I wonder if Margaret Gordon could have been quite sane. It is strange that Neil has never told her the truth. Perhaps he doesn't want her to find out."

Eric had met Neil Gordon a few evenings before this, at a country dance where Neil had played the violin for the dancers. Influenced by curiosity he had sought the lad's acquaintance. Neil was friendly and talkative at first; but at the first hint concerning the Gordons which Eric threw out skilfully his face and manner changed. He looked secretive and suspicious, almost sinister. A sullen look crept into his big black eyes and he drew his bow across the violin strings with a discordant screech, as if to terminate the conversation. Plainly nothing was to be found out from him about Kilmeny and her grim guardians.

A TROUBLING OF THE WATERS

One evening in late June Mrs. Williamson was sitting by her kitchen window. Her knitting lay unheeded in her lap, and Timothy, though he nestled ingratiatingly against her foot as he lay on the rug and purred his loudest, was unregarded. She rested her face on her hand and looked out of the window, across the distant harbour, with troubled eyes.

"I guess I must speak," she thought wistfully. "I hate to do it. I always did hate meddling. My mother always used to say that ninety-nine times out of a hundred the last state of a meddler and them she meddled with was worse than the first. But I guess it's my duty. I was Margaret's friend, and it is my duty to protect her child any way I can. If the Master does go back across there to meet her I must tell him what I think about it."

Overhead in his room, Eric was walking about whistling. Presently he came downstairs, thinking of the orchard, and the girl who would be waiting for him there.

As he crossed the little front entry he heard Mrs. Williamson's voice calling to him.

"Mr. Marshall, will you please come here a moment?"

He went out to the kitchen. Mrs. Williamson looked at him deprecatingly. There was a flush on her faded cheek and her voice trembled.

"Mr. Marshall, I want to ask you a question. Perhaps you will think it isn't any of my business. But it isn't because I want to meddle. No, no. It is only because I think I ought to speak. I have thought it over for a long time, and it seems to me that I ought to speak. I hope you won't be angry, but even if you are I must say what I have to say. Are you going back to the old Connors orchard to meet Kilmeny Gordon?"

For a moment an angry flush burned in Eric's face. It was more Mrs. Williamson's tone than her words which startled and annoyed him.

59

"Yes, I am, Mrs. Williamson," he said coldly. "What of it?"

"Then, sir," said Mrs. Williamson with more firmness, "I have got to tell you that I don't think you are doing right. I have been suspecting all along that that was where you went every evening, but I haven't said a word to any one about it. Even my husband doesn't know. But tell me this, Master. Do Kilmeny's uncle and aunt know that you are meeting her there?"

"Why," said Eric, in some confusion, "I—I do not know whether they do or not. But Mrs. Williamson, surely you do not suspect me of meaning any harm or wrong to Kilmeny Gordon?"

"No, I don't, Master. I might think it of some men, but never of you. I don't for a minute think that you would do her or any woman any wilful wrong. But you may do her great harm for all that. I want you to stop and think about it. I guess you haven't thought. Kilmeny can't know anything about the world or about men, and she may get to thinking too much of you. That might break her heart, because you couldn't ever marry a dumb girl like her. So I don't think you ought to be meeting her so often in this fashion. It isn't right, Master. Don't go to the orchard again."

Without a word Eric turned away, and went upstairs to his room. Mrs. Williamson picked up her knitting with a sigh.

"That's done, Timothy, and I'm real thankful," she said. "I guess there'll be no need of saying anything more. Mr. Marshall is a fine young man, only a little thoughtless. Now that he's got his eyes opened I'm sure he'll do what is right. I don't want Margaret's child made unhappy."

Her husband came to the kitchen door and sat down on the steps to enjoy his evening smoke, talking between whiffs to his wife of Elder Tracy's church row, and Mary Alice Martin's beau, the price Jake Crosby was giving for eggs, the quantity of hay yielded by the hill meadow, the trouble he was having with old Molly's calf, and the respective merits of Plymouth Rock and Brahma roosters. Mrs. Williamson answered at random, and heard not one word in ten.

"What's got the Master, Mother?" inquired old Robert, presently. "I hear him striding up and down in his room 'sif he was caged. Sure you didn't lock him in by mistake?"

"Maybe he's worried over the way Seth Tracy's acting in school," suggested Mrs. Williamson, who did not choose that her gossipy husband should suspect the truth about Eric and Kilmeny Gordon.

"Shucks, he needn't worry a morsel over that. Seth'll quiet down as soon as he finds he can't run the Master. He's a rare good teacher—better'n Mr. West was even, and that's saying something. The trustees are hoping he'll stay for another term. They're going to ask him at the school meeting to-morrow, and offer him a raise of supplement."

Upstairs, in his little room under the eaves, Eric Marshall was in the grip of the most intense and overwhelming emotion he had ever experienced.

Up and down, to and fro, he walked, with set lips and clenched hands. When he was wearied out he flung himself on a chair by the window and wrestled with the flood of feeling.

Mrs. Williamson's words had torn away the delusive veil with which he had bound his eyes. He was face to face with the knowledge that he loved Kilmeny Gordon with the love that comes but once, and is for all time. He wondered how he could have been so long blind to it. He knew that he must have loved her ever since their first meeting that May evening in the old orchard.

And he knew that he must choose between two alternatives—either he must never go to the orchard again, or he must go as an avowed lover to woo him a wife.

Worldly prudence, his inheritance from a long line of thrifty, cool-headed ancestors, was strong in Eric, and he did not yield easily or speedily to the dictates of his passion. All night he struggled against the new emotions that threatened to sweep away the "common sense" which David Baker had bade him take with him when he went a-wooing. Would not a marriage with Kilmeny Gordon be an unwise thing from any standpoint?

Then something stronger and greater and more vital than wisdom or unwisdom rose up in him and mastered him. Kilmeny, beautiful, dumb Kilmeny was, as he had once involuntarily thought, "the one maid" for him. Nothing should part them. The mere idea of never seeing her again was so unbearable that he laughed at himself for having counted it a possible alternative.

"If I can win Kilmeny's love I shall ask her to be my wife," he said, looking out of the window to the dark, southwestern hill beyond which lay his orchard.

The velvet sky over it was still starry; but the water of the harbour was beginning to grow silvery in the reflection of the dawn that was breaking in the east.

"Her misfortune will only make her dearer to me. I cannot realize that a month ago I did not know her. It seems to me that she has been a part of my life for ever. I wonder if she was grieved that I did not go to the orchard last night—if she waited for me. If she does, she does not know it herself yet. It will be my sweet task to teach her what love means, and no man has ever had a lovelier, purer, pupil."

At the annual school meeting, the next afternoon, the trustees asked Eric to take the Lindsay school for the following year. He consented unhesitatingly. That evening he went to Mrs. Williamson, as she washed her tea dishes in the kitchen.

"Mrs. Williamson, I am going back to the old Connors orchard to see Kilmeny again to-night."

She looked at him reproachfully.

"Well, Master, I have no more to say. I suppose it wouldn't be of any use if I had. But you know what I think of it."

"I intend to marry Kilmeny Gordon if I can win her."

An expression of amazement came into the good woman's face. She looked scrutinizingly at the firm mouth and steady gray eyes for a moment. Then she said in a troubled voice,

"Do you think that is wise, Master? I suppose Kilmeny is pretty; the egg peddler told me she was; and no doubt she is a good, nice girl. But she wouldn't be a suitable wife for you—a girl that can't speak."

"That doesn't make any difference to me."

"But what will your people say?"

"I have no 'people' except my father. When he sees Kilmeny he will understand. She is all the world to me, Mrs. Williamson."

"As long as you believe that there is nothing more to be said," was the quiet answer, "I'd be a little bit afraid if I was you, though. But young people never think of those things."

"My only fear is that she won't care for me," said Eric soberly.

Mrs. Williamson surveyed the handsome, broad-shouldered young man shrewdly.

"I don't think there are many women would say you 'no', Master. I wish you well in your wooing, though I can't help thinking you're doing a daft-like thing. I hope you won't have any trouble with Thomas and Janet. They are so different from other folks there is no knowing. But take my advice, Master, and go and see them about it right off. Don't go on meeting Kilmeny unbeknownst to them."

"I shall certainly take your advice," said Eric, gravely. "I should have gone to them before. It was merely thoughtlessness on my part. Possibly they do know already. Kilmeny may have told them."

Mrs. Williamson shook her head decidedly.

"No, no, Master, she hasn't. They'd never have let her go on meeting you there if they had known. I know them too well to think of that for a moment. Go you straight to them and say to them just what you have said to me. That is your best plan, Master. And take care of Neil. People say he has a notion of Kilmeny himself. He'll do you a bad turn if he can, I've no doubt. Them foreigners can't be trusted—and he's just as much a foreigner as his parents before him—though he HAS been brought up on oatmeal and the shorter catechism, as the old saying has it. I feel that somehow—I always feel it when I look at him singing in the choir."

"Oh, I am not afraid of Neil," said Eric carelessly. "He couldn't help loving Kilmeny—nobody could."

"I suppose every young man thinks that about his girl—if he's the right sort of young man," said Mrs. Williamson with a little sigh.

She watched Eric out of sight anxiously.

"I hope it'll all come out right," she thought. "I hope he ain't making an awful mistake—but—I'm afraid. Kilmeny must be very pretty to have bewitched him so. Well, I suppose there is no use in my worrying over it. But I do wish he had never gone back to that old orchard and seen her."

A LOVER AND HIS LASS

Kilmeny was in the orchard when Eric reached it, and he lingered for a moment in the shadow of the spruce wood to dream over her beauty.

The orchard had lately overflowed in waves of old-fashioned caraway, and she was standing in the midst of its sea of bloom, with the lace-like blossoms swaying around her in the wind. She wore the simple dress of pale blue print in which he had first seen her; silk attire could not better have become her loveliness. She had woven herself a chaplet of half open white rosebuds and placed it on her dark hair, where the delicate blossoms seemed less wonderful than her face.

When Eric stepped through the gap she ran to meet him with outstretched hands, smiling. He took her hands and looked into her eyes with an expression before which hers for the first time faltered. She looked down, and a warm blush strained the ivory curves of her cheek and throat. His heart bounded, for in that blush he recognized the banner of love's vanguard.

"Are you glad to see me, Kilmeny?" he asked, in a low significant tone.

She nodded, and wrote in a somewhat embarrassed fashion,

"Yes. Why do you ask? You know I am always glad to see you. I was afraid you would not come. You did not come last night and I was so sorry. Nothing in the orchard seemed nice any longer. I couldn't even play. I tried to, and my violin only cried. I waited until it was dark and then I went home."

"I am sorry you were disappointed, Kilmeny. I couldn't come last night. Some day I shall tell you why. I stayed home to learn a new lesson. I am sorry you missed me—no, I am glad. Can you understand how a person may be glad and sorry for the same thing?"

She nodded again, with a return of her usual sweet composure.

"Yes, I could not have understood once, but I can now. Did you learn your new lesson?"

"Yes, very thoroughly. It was a delightful lesson when I once understood it. I must try to teach it to you some day. Come over to the old bench, Kilmeny. There is something I want to say to you. But first, will you give me a rose?"

She ran to the bush, and, after careful deliberation, selected a perfect half-open bud and brought it to him—a white bud with a faint, sunrise flush about its golden heart.

"Thank you. It is as beautiful as—as a woman I know," Eric said.

A wistful look came into her face at his words, and she walked with a drooping head across the orchard to the bench.

"Kilmeny," he said, seriously, "I am going to ask you to do something for me. I want you to take me home with you and introduce me to your uncle and aunt."

She lifted her head and stared at him incredulously, as if he had asked her to do something wildly impossible. Understanding from his grave face that he meant what he said, a look of dismay dawned in her eyes. She shook her head almost violently and seemed to be making a passionate, instinctive effort to speak. Then she caught up her pencil and wrote with feverish haste:

"I cannot do that. Do not ask me to. You do not understand. They would be very angry. They do not want to see any one coming to the house. And they would never let me come here again. Oh, you do not mean it?"

He pitied her for the pain and bewilderment in her eyes; but he took her slender hands in his and said firmly,

"Yes, Kilmeny, I do mean it. It is not quite right for us to be meeting each other here as we have been doing, without the knowledge and consent of your friends. You cannot now understand this, but—believe me—it is so."

She looked questioningly, pityingly into his eyes. What she read there seemed to convince her, for she turned very pale and an expression of hopelessness came into her face. Releasing her hands, she wrote slowly,

"If you say it is wrong I must believe it. I did not know anything so pleasant could be wrong. But if it is wrong we must not meet here any more. Mother told me I must never do anything that was wrong. But I did not know this was wrong."

"It was not wrong for you, Kilmeny. But it was a little wrong for me, because I knew better—or rather, should have known better. I didn't stop to think, as the children say. Some day you will understand fully. Now, you will take me to your uncle and aunt, and after I have said to them what I want to say it will be all right for us to meet here or anywhere."

She shook her head.

"No," she wrote, "Uncle Thomas and Aunt Janet will tell you to go away and never come back. And they will never let me come here any more. Since it is not right to meet you I will not come, but it is no use to think of going to them. I did not tell them about you because I knew that they would forbid me to see you, but I am sorry, since it is so wrong."

"You must take me to them," said Eric firmly. "I am quite sure that things will not be as you fear when they hear what I have to say."

Uncomforted, she wrote forlornly,

"I must do it, since you insist, but I am sure it will be no use. I cannot take you to-night because they are away. They went to the store at Radnor. But I will take you to-morrow night; and after that I shall not see you any more."

Two great tears brimmed over in her big blue eyes and splashed down on her slate. Her lips quivered like a hurt child's. Eric put his arm impulsively about her and drew her head down upon his shoulder. As she cried there, softly, miserably, he pressed his lips to the silky black hair with its coronal of rosebuds. He did not see two burning eyes which were looking at him over the old fence behind him with hatred and mad passion blazing in their depths. Neil Gordon was crouched there, with clenched hands and heaving breast, watching them.

"Kilmeny, dear, don't cry," said Eric tenderly. "You shall see me again. I promise you that, whatever happens. I do not think your uncle and aunt will be as unreasonable as you fear, but even if they are they shall not prevent me from meeting you somehow."

Kilmeny lifted her head, and wiped the tears from her eyes.

"You do not know what they are like," she wrote. "They will lock me into my room. That is the way they always punished me when I was a little girl. And once, not so very long ago, when I was a big girl, they did it."

"If they do I'll get you out somehow," said Eric, laughing a little.

She allowed herself to smile, but it was a rather forlorn little effort. She did not cry any more, but her spirits did not come back to her. Eric talked gaily, but she only listened in a pensive, absent way, as if she scarcely heard him. When he asked her to play she shook her head.

"I cannot think any music to-night," she wrote, "I must go home, for my head aches and I feel very stupid."

"Very well, Kilmeny. Now, don't worry, little girl. It will all come out all right."

Evidently she did not share his confidence, for her head drooped again as they walked together across the orchard. At the entrance of the wild cherry lane she paused and looked at him half reproachfully, her eyes filling again. She seemed to be bidding him a mute farewell. With an impulse of tenderness which he could not control, Eric put his arm about her and kissed her red, trembling mouth. She started back with a little cry. A burning colour swept over her face, and the next moment she fled swiftly up the darkening lane.

The sweetness of that involuntary kiss clung to Eric's lips as he went homeward, half-intoxicating him. He knew that it had opened the gates of womanhood to Kilmeny. Never again, he felt, would her eyes meet his with their old unclouded frankness. When next he looked into them he knew that he should see there the consciousness of his kiss. Behind her in the orchard that night Kilmeny had left her childhood.

A PRISONER OF LOVE

When Eric betook himself to the orchard the next evening he had to admit that he felt rather nervous. He did not know how the Gordons would receive him and certainly the reports he had heard of them were not encouraging, to say the least of it. Even Mrs. Williamson, when he had told her where he was going, seemed to look upon him as one bent on bearding a lion in his den.

"I do hope they won't be very uncivil to you, Master," was the best she could say.

He expected Kilmeny to be in the orchard before him, for he had been delayed by a call from one of the trustees; but she was nowhere to be seen. He walked across it to the wild cherry lane; but at its entrance he stopped short in sudden dismay.

Neil Gordon had stepped from behind the trees and stood confronting him, with blazing eyes, and lips which writhed in emotion so great that at first it prevented him from speaking.

With a thrill of dismay Eric instantly understood what must have taken place. Neil had discovered that he and Kilmeny had been meeting in the orchard, and beyond doubt had carried that tale to Janet and Thomas Gordon. He realized how unfortunate it was that this should have happened before he had had time to make his own explanation. It would probably prejudice Kilmeny's guardians still further against him. At this point in his thoughts Neil's pent up passion suddenly found vent in a burst of wild words.

"So you've come to meet her again. But she isn't here—you'll never see her again! I hate you—I hate you—I hate you!"

His voice rose to a shrill scream. He took a furious step nearer Eric as if he would attack him. Eric looked steadily in his eyes with a calm defiance, before which his wild passion broke like foam on a rock.

"So you have been making trouble for Kilmeny, Neil, have you?" said Eric contemptuously. "I suppose you have been playing the spy. And I suppose that you have told her uncle and aunt that she has been meeting me here. Well, you have saved me the trouble of doing it, that is all. I was going to tell them myself, tonight. I don't know what your motive in doing this has been. Was it jealousy of me? Or have you done it out of malice to Kilmeny?"

His contempt cowed Neil more effectually than any display of anger could have done.

"Never you mind why I did it," he muttered sullenly. "What I did or why I did it is no business of yours. And you have no business to come sneaking around here either. Kilmeny won't meet you here again."

"She will meet me in her own home then," said Eric sternly. "Neil, in behaving as you have done you have shown yourself to be a very foolish, undisciplined boy. I am going straightway to Kilmeny's uncle and aunt to explain everything."

Neil sprang forward in his path.

"No—no—go away," he implored wildly. "Oh, sir—oh, Mr. Marshall, please go away. I'll do anything for you if you will. I love Kilmeny. I've loved her all my life. I'd give my life for her. I can't have you coming here to steal her from me. If you do—I'll kill you! I wanted to kill you last night when I saw you kiss her. Oh, yes, I saw you. I was watching—spying, if you like. I don't care what you call it. I had followed her—I suspected something. She was so different—so changed. She never would wear the flowers I picked for her any more. She seemed to forget I was there. I knew something had come between us. And it was you, curse you! Oh, I'll make you sorry for it."

He was working himself up into a fury again—the untamed fury of the Italian peasant thwarted in his heart's desire. It overrode all the restraint of his training and environment. Eric, amid all his anger and annoyance, felt a thrill of pity for him. Neil Gordon was only a boy still; and he was miserable and beside himself.

"Neil, listen to me," he said quietly. "You are talking very foolishly. It is not for you to say who shall or shall not be Kilmeny's friend. Now, you may just as well control yourself and go home like a decent fellow. I am not at all frightened by your threats, and I shall know how to deal with you if you persist in interfering with me or persecuting Kilmeny. I am not the sort of person to put up with that, my lad."

The restrained power in his tone and look cowed Neil. The latter turned sullenly away, with another muttered curse, and plunged into the shadow of the firs.

Eric, not a little ruffled under all his external composure by this most unexpected and unpleasant encounter, pursued his way along the lane which wound on by the belt of woodland in twist and curve to the Gordon homestead. His heart beat as he thought of Kilmeny. What might she not be suffering? Doubtless Neil had given a very exaggerated and distorted account of what he had seen, and probably her dour relations were very angry with her, poor child. Anxious to avert their wrath as soon as might be, he hurried on, almost forgetting his meeting with Neil. The threats of the latter did not trouble him at all. He thought the angry outburst of a jealous boy mattered but little. What did matter was that Kilmeny was in trouble which his heedlessness had brought upon her.

Presently he found himself before the Gordon house. It was an old building with sharp eaves and dormer windows, its shingles stained a dark gray by long exposure to wind and weather. Faded green shutters hung on the windows of the lower story. Behind it grew a thick wood of spruces. The little yard in front of it was grassy and prim and flowerless; but over the low front door a luxuriant early-flowering rose vine clambered, in a riot of blood-red blossom which contrasted strangely with the general bareness of its surroundings. It seemed to fling itself over the grim old house as if intent on bombarding it with an alien life and joyousness.

Eric knocked at the door, wondering if it might be possible that Kilmeny should come to it. But a moment later it was opened by an elderly woman—a woman of rigid lines from the hem of her lank, dark print dress to the crown of her head, covered with black hair which, despite its few gray threads, was still thick and luxuriant. She had a long, pale face somewhat worn and wrinkled, but possessing a certain harsh comeliness of feature which neither age nor wrinkles had quite destroyed; and her deep-set, light gray eyes were not devoid of suggested kindliness, although they now surveyed Eric with an unconcealed hostility. Her figure, in its merciless dress, was very angular; yet there was about her a dignity of carriage and manner which Eric liked. In any case, he preferred her unsmiling dourness to vulgar garrulity.

He lifted his hat.

"Have I the honour of speaking to Miss Gordon?" he asked.

"I am Janet Gordon," said the woman stiffly.

"Then I wish to talk with you and your brother."

"Come in."

She stepped aside and motioned him to a low brown door opening on the right.

"Go in and sit down. I'll call Thomas," she said coldly, as she walked out through the hall.

Eric walked into the parlour and sat down as bidden. He found himself in the most old-fashioned room he had ever seen. The solidly made chairs and tables, of some wood grown dark and polished with age, made even Mrs.

71

Williamson's "parlour set" of horsehair seem extravagantly modern by contrast. The painted floor was covered with round braided rugs. On the centre table was a lamp, a Bible and some theological volumes contemporary with the square-runged furniture. The walls, wainscoted half way up in wood and covered for the rest with a dark, diamond-patterned paper, were hung with faded engravings, mostly of clerical-looking, bewigged personages in gowns and bands.

But over the high, undecorated black mantel-piece, in a ruddy glow of sunset light striking through the window, hung one which caught and held Eric's attention to the exclusion of everything else. It was the enlarged "crayon" photograph of a young girl, and, in spite of the crudity of execution, it was easily the center of interest in the room.

Eric at once guessed that this must be the picture of Margaret Gordon, for, although quite unlike Kilmeny's sensitive, spirited face in general, there was a subtle, unmistakable resemblance about brow and chin.

The pictured face was a very handsome one, suggestive of velvety dark eyes and vivid colouring; but it was its expression rather than its beauty which fascinated Eric. Never had he seen a countenance indicative of more intense and stubborn will power. Margaret Gordon was dead and buried; the picture was a cheap and inartistic production in an impossible frame of gilt and plush; yet the vitality in that face dominated its surroundings still. What then must have been the power of such a personality in life?

Eric realized that this woman could and would have done whatsoever she willed, unflinchingly and unrelentingly. She could stamp her desire on everything and everybody about her, moulding them to her wish and will, in their own despite and in defiance of all the resistance they might make. Many things in Kilmeny's upbringing and temperament became clear to him.

"If that woman had told me I was ugly I should have believed her," he thought. "Ay, even though I had a mirror to contradict her. I should never have dreamed of disputing or questioning anything she might have said. The strange power in her face is almost uncanny, peering out as it does from a mask of beauty and youthful curves. Pride and stubbornness are its salient characteristics. Well, Kilmeny does not at all resemble her mother in expression and only very slightly in feature."

His reflections were interrupted by the entrance of Thomas and Janet Gordon. The former had evidently been called from his work. He nodded without speaking, and the two sat gravely down before Eric.

"I have come to see you with regard to your niece, Mr. Gordon," he said abruptly, realizing that there would be small use in beating about the bush with this grim pair. "I met your—I met Neil Gordon in the Connors orchard, and I found that he has told you that I have been meeting Kilmeny there."

He paused. Thomas Gordon nodded again; but he did not speak, and he did not remove his steady, piercing eyes from the young man's flushed countenance. Janet still sat in a sort of expectant immovability.

"I fear that you have formed an unfavourable opinion of me on this account, Mr. Gordon," Eric went on. "But I hardly think I deserve it. I can explain the matter if you will allow me. I met your niece accidentally in the orchard three weeks ago and heard her play. I thought her music very wonderful and I fell into the habit of coming to the orchard in the evenings to hear it. I had no thought of harming her in any way, Mr. Gordon. I thought of her as a mere child, and a child who was doubly sacred because of her affliction. But recently I—I—it occurred to me that I was not behaving quite honourably in encouraging her to meet me thus. Yesterday evening I asked her to bring me here and introduce me to you and her aunt. We would have come then if you had been at home. As you were not we arranged to come tonight."

"I hope you will not refuse me the privilege of seeing your niece, Mr. Gordon," said Eric eagerly. "I ask you to allow me to visit her here. But I do not ask you to receive me as a friend on my own recommendations only. I will give you references—men of standing in Charlottetown and Queenslea. If you refer to them—"

"I don't need to do that," said Thomas Gordon, quietly. "I know more of you than you think, Master. I know your father well by reputation and I have seen him. I know you are a rich man's son, whatever your whim in teaching a country school may be. Since you have kept your own counsel about your affairs I supposed you didn't want your true position generally known, and so I have held my tongue about you. I know no ill of you, Master, and I think none, now that I believe you were not beguiling Kilmeny to meet you unknown to her friends of set purpose. But all this doesn't make you a suitable friend for her, sir—it makes you all the more unsuitable. The less she sees of you the better."

Eric almost started to his feet in an indignant protest; but he swiftly remembered that his only hope of winning Kilmeny lay in bringing Thomas Gordon to another way of thinking. He had got on better than he had expected so far; he must not now jeopardize what he had gained by rashness or impatience.

"Why do you think so, Mr. Gordon?" he asked, regaining his self-control with an effort.

"Well, plain speaking is best, Master. If you were to come here and see Kilmeny often she'd most likely come to think too much of you. I mistrust there's some mischief done in that direction already. Then when you went away she might break her heart—for she is one of those who feel things deeply. She has been happy enough. I know folks condemn us for the way she has been brought up, but they don't know everything. It was the best way for her, all things considered. And we don't want her made unhappy, Master."

"But I love your niece and I want to marry her if I can win her love," said Eric steadily.

He surprised them out of their self possession at last. Both started, and looked at him as if they could not believe the evidence of their ears.

"Marry her! Marry Kilmeny!" exclaimed Thomas Gordon incredulously. "You can't mean it, sir. Why, she is dumb—Kilmeny is dumb."

"That makes no difference in my love for her, although I deeply regret it for her own sake," answered Eric. "I can only repeat what I have already said, Mr. Gordon. I want Kilmeny for my wife."

The older man leaned forward and looked at the floor in a troubled fashion, drawing his bushy eyebrows down and tapping the calloused tips of his fingers together uneasily. He was evidently puzzled by this unexpected turn of the conversation, and in grave doubt what to say.

"What would your father say to all this, Master?" he queried at last.

"I have often heard my father say that a man must marry to please himself," said Eric, with a smile. "If he felt tempted to go back on that opinion I think the sight of Kilmeny would convert him. But, after all, it is what I say that matters in this case, isn't it, Mr. Gordon? I am well educated and not afraid of work. I can make a home for Kilmeny in a few years even if I have to depend entirely on my own resources. Only give me the chance to win her—that is all I ask."

"I don't think it would do, Master," said Thomas Gordon, shaking his head. "Of course, I dare say you—you"—he tried to say "love," but Scotch reserve balked stubbornly at the terrible word—"you think you like Kilmeny now, but you are only a lad—and lads' fancies change."

"Mine will not," Eric broke in vehemently. "It is not a fancy, Mr. Gordon. It is the love that comes once in a lifetime and once only. I may be but a lad, but I know that Kilmeny is the one woman in the world for me. There can never be any other. Oh, I'm not speaking rashly or inconsiderately. I have weighed the matter well and looked at it from every aspect. And it all comes to this—I love Kilmeny and I want what any decent man who loves a woman truly has the right to have—the chance to win her love in return."

"Well!" Thomas Gordon drew a long breath that was almost a sigh. "Maybe—if you feel like that, Master—I don't know—there are some things it isn't right to cross. Perhaps we oughtn't—Janet, woman, what shall we say to him?"

Janet Gordon had hitherto spoken no word. She had sat rigidly upright on one of the old chairs under Margaret Gordon's insistent picture, with her knotted, toil-worn hands grasping the carved arms tightly, and her eyes fastened on Eric's face. At first their expression had been guarded and hostile, but as the conversation proceeded they lost this gradually and became almost kindly. Now, when her brother appealed to her, she leaned forward and said eagerly,

"Do you know that there is a stain on Kilmeny's birth, Master?"

"I know that her mother was the innocent victim of a very sad mistake, Miss Gordon. I admit no real stain where there was no conscious wrong doing. Though, for that matter, even if there were, it would be no fault of Kilmeny's and would make no difference to me as far as she is concerned."

A sudden change swept over Janet Gordon's face, quite marvelous in the transformation it wrought. Her grim mouth softened and a flood of repressed tenderness glorified her cold gray eyes.

"Well, then." she said almost triumphantly, "since neither that nor her dumbness seems to be any drawback in your eyes I don't see why you should not have the chance you want. Perhaps your world will say she is not good enough for you, but she is—she is"—this half defiantly. "She is a sweet and innocent and true-hearted lassie. She is bright and clever and she is not ill looking. Thomas, I say let the young man have his will."

Thomas Gordon stood up, as if he considered the responsibility off his shoulders and the interview at an end.

"Very well, Janet, woman, since you think it is wise. And may God deal with him as he deals with her. Good evening, Master. I'll see you again, and you are free to come and go as suits you. But I must go to my work now. I left my horses standing in the field."

"I will go up and send Kilmeny down," said Janet quietly.

She lighted the lamp on the table and left the room. A few minutes later Kilmeny came down. Eric rose and went to meet her eagerly, but she only put out her right hand with a pretty dignity and, while she looked into his face, she did not look into his eyes.

"You see I was right after all, Kilmeny," he said, smiling. "Your uncle and aunt haven't driven me away. On the contrary they have been very kind to me, and they say I may see you whenever and wherever I like."

She smiled, and went over to the table to write on her slate.

"But they were very angry last night, and said dreadful things to me. I felt very frightened and unhappy. They seemed to think I had done something terribly wrong. Uncle Thomas said he would never trust me out of his sight again. I could hardly believe it when Aunt Janet came up and told me you were here and that I might come down. She looked at me very strangely as she spoke, but I could see that all the anger had gone out of her face. She seemed pleased and yet sad. But I am glad they have forgiven us."

She did not tell him how glad she was, and how unhappy she had been over the thought that she was never to see him again. Yesterday she would have told him all frankly and fully; but for her yesterday was a lifetime away—a lifetime in which she had come into her heritage of womanly dignity and reserve. The kiss which Eric had left on her lips, the words her uncle and aunt had said to her, the tears she had shed for the first time on a sleepless pillow—all had conspired to reveal her to herself. She did not yet dream that she loved Eric Marshall, or that he loved her. But she was no longer the child to be made a dear comrade of. She was, though quite unconsciously, the woman to be wooed and won, exacting, with sweet, innate pride, her dues of allegiance.

A SWEETER WOMAN NE'ER DREW BREATH

Thenceforward Eric Marshall was a constant visitor at the Gordon homestead. He soon became a favourite with Thomas and Janet, especially the latter. He liked them both, discovering under all their outward peculiarities sterling worth and fitness of character. Thomas Gordon was surprisingly well read and could floor Eric any time in argument, once he became sufficiently warmed up to attain fluency of words. Eric hardly recognized him the first time he saw him thus animated. His bent form straightened, his sunken eyes flashed, his face flushed, his voice rang like a trumpet, and he poured out a flood of eloquence which swept Eric's smart, up-to-date arguments away like straws in the rush of a mountain torrent. Eric enjoyed his own defeat enormously, but Thomas Gordon was ashamed of being thus drawn out of himself, and for a week afterwards confined his remarks to "Yes" and "No," or, at the outside, to a brief statement that a change in the weather was brewing.

Janet never talked on matters of church and state; such she plainly considered to be far beyond a woman's province. But she listened with lurking interest in her eyes while Thomas and Eric pelted on each other with facts and statistics and opinions, and on the rare occasions when Eric scored a point she permitted herself a sly little smile at her brother's expense.

Of Neil, Eric saw but little. The Italian boy avoided him, or if they chanced to meet passed him by with sullen, downcast eyes. Eric did not trouble himself greatly about Neil; but Thomas Gordon, understanding the motive which had led Neil to betray his discovery of the orchard trysts, bluntly told Kilmeny that she must not make such an equal of Neil as she had done.

"You have been too kind to the lad, lassie, and he's got presumptuous. He must be taught his place. I mistrust we have all made more of him than we should."

But most of the idyllic hours of Eric's wooing were spent in the old orchard; the garden end of it was now a wilderness of roses—roses red as the heart of a sunset, roses pink as the early flush of dawn, roses white as the snows on mountain peaks, roses full blown, and roses in buds that were sweeter than anything on earth except Kilmeny's face. Their petals fell in silken heaps along the old paths or clung to the lush grasses among which Eric lay and dreamed, while Kilmeny played to him on her violin.

Eric promised himself that when she was his wife her wonderful gift for music should be cultivated to the utmost. Her powers of expression seemed to deepen and develop every day, growing as her soul grew, taking on new colour and richness from her ripening heart.

To Eric, the days were all pages in an inspired idyl. He had never dreamed that love could be so mighty or the world so beautiful. He wondered if the universe were big enough to hold his joy or eternity long enough to live it out. His whole existence was, for the time being, bounded by that orchard where he wooed his sweetheart. All other ambitions and plans and hopes were set aside in the pursuit of this one aim, the attainment of which would enhance all others a thousand-fold, the loss of which would rob all others of their reason for existence. His own world seemed very far away and the things of that world forgotten.

His father, on hearing that he had taken the Lindsay school for a year, had written him a testy, amazed letter, asking him if he were demented.

"Or is there a girl in the case?" he wrote. "There must be, to tie you down to a place like Lindsay for a year. Take care, master Eric; you've been too sensible all your life. A man is bound to make a fool of himself at least once, and when you didn't get through with that in your teens it may be attacking you now."

David also wrote, expostulating more gravely; but he did not express the suspicions Eric knew he must entertain.

"Good old David! He is quaking with fear that I am up to something he can't approve of, but he won't say a word by way of attempting to force my confidence."

It could not long remain a secret in Lindsay that "the Master" was going to the Gordon place on courting thoughts intent. Mrs. Williamson kept her own and Eric's counsel; the Gordons said nothing; but the secret leaked out and great was the surprise and gossip and wonder. One or two incautious people ventured to express their opinion of the Master's wisdom to the Master himself; but they never repeated the experiment. Curiosity was rife. A hundred stories were circulated about Kilmeny, all greatly exaggerated in the circulation. Wise heads were shaken and the majority opined that it was a great pity. The Master was a likely young fellow; he could have his pick of almost anybody, you might think; it was too bad that he should go and take up with that queer, dumb niece of the Gordons who had been brought up in such a heathenish way. But then you never could guess what way a man's fancy would jump when he set out to pick him a wife. They guessed Neil Gordon didn't like it much. He seemed to have got dreadful moody and sulky of late and wouldn't sing in the choir any more. Thus the buzz of comment and gossip ran.

To those two in the old orchard it mattered not a whit. Kilmeny knew nothing of gossip. To her, Lindsay was as much of an unknown world as the city of Eric's home. Her thoughts strayed far and wide in the realm of her fancy, but they never wandered out to the little realities that hedged her strange life around. In that life she had blossomed out, a fair, unique thing. There were times when Eric almost regretted that one day he must take her out of her white solitude to a world that, in the last analysis, was only Lindsay on a larger scale, with just the same pettiness of thought and feeling and opinion at the bottom of it. He wished he might keep her to himself for ever, in that old, spruce-hidden orchard where the roses fell.

One day he indulged himself in the fulfillment of the whim he had formed when Kilmeny had told him she thought herself ugly. He went to Janet and asked her permission to bring a mirror to the house that he might have the privilege of being the first to reveal Kilmeny to herself exteriorly. Janet was somewhat dubious at first.

"There hasn't been such a thing in the house for sixteen years, Master. There never was but three—one in the spare room, and a little one in the kitchen, and Margaret's own. She broke them all the day it first struck her that Kilmeny was going to be bonny. I might have got one after she died maybe. But I didn't think of it; and there's no need of lasses to be always prinking at their looking glasses."

But Eric pleaded and argued skilfully, and finally Janet said,

"Well, well, have your own way. You'd have it anyway I think, lad. You are one of those men who always get their own way. But that is different from the men who TAKE their own way—and that's a mercy," she added under her breath.

Eric went to town the next Saturday and picked out a mirror that pleased him. He had it shipped to Radnor and Thomas Gordon brought it home, not knowing what it was, for Janet had thought it just as well he should not know.

"It's a present the Master is making Kilmeny," she told him.

She sent Kilmeny off to the orchard after tea, and Eric slipped around to the house by way of the main road and lane. He and Janet together unpacked the mirror and hung it on the parlour wall.

"I never saw such a big one, Master," said Janet rather doubtfully, as if, after all, she distrusted its gleaming, pearly depth and richly ornamented frame. "I hope it won't make her vain. She is very bonny, but it may not do her any good to know it."

"It won't harm her," said Eric confidently. "When a belief in her ugliness hasn't spoiled a girl a belief in her beauty won't."

But Janet did not understand epigrams. She carefully removed a little dust from the polished surface, and frowned meditatively at the by no means beautiful reflection she saw therein.

"I cannot think what made Kilmeny suppose she was ugly, Master."

"Her mother told her she was," said Eric, rather bitterly.

"Ah!" Janet shot a quick glance at the picture of her sister. "Was that it? Margaret was a strange woman, Master. I suppose she thought her own beauty had been a snare to her. She WAS bonny. That picture doesn't do her justice. I never liked it. It was taken before she was—before she met Ronald Fraser. We none of us thought it very like her at the time. But, Master, three years later it was like her—oh, it was like her then! That very look came in her face."

"Kilmeny doesn't resemble her mother," remarked Eric, glancing at the picture with the same feeling of mingled fascination and distaste with which he always regarded it. "Does she look like her father?"

"No, not a great deal, though some of her ways are very like his. She looks like her grandmother—Margaret's mother, Master. Her name was Kilmeny too, and she was a handsome, sweet woman. I was very fond of my stepmother, Master. When she died she gave her baby to me, and asked me to be a mother to it. Ah well, I tried; but I couldn't fence the sorrow out of Margaret's life, and it sometimes comes to my mind that maybe I'll not be able to fence it out of Kilmeny's either."

"That will be my task," said Eric.

"You'll do your best, I do not doubt. But maybe it will be through you that sorrow will come to her after all."

"Not through any fault of mine, Aunt Janet."

"No, no, I'm not saying it will be your fault. But my heart misgives me at times. Oh, I dare say I am only a foolish old woman, Master. Go your ways and bring your lass here to look at your plaything when you like. I'll not make or meddle with it."

Janet betook herself to the kitchen and Eric went to look for Kilmeny. She was not in the orchard and it was not until he had searched for some time that he found her. She was standing under a beech tree in a field beyond the orchard, leaning on the longer fence, with her hands clasped against her cheek. In them she held a white Mary-lily from the orchard. She did not run to meet him while he was crossing the pasture, as she would once have done. She waited motionless until he was close to her. Eric began, half laughingly, half tenderly, to quote some lines from her namesake ballad:

"'Kilmeny, Kilmeny, where have you been?
Long hae we sought baith holt and den,—

By linn, by ford, and greenwood tree!
Yet you are halesome and fair to see.
Where got you that joup o' the lily sheen?
That bonny snood o' the birk sae green,
And those roses, the fairest that ever was seen?
Kilmeny, Kilmeny, where have you been?'
"Only it's a lily and not a rose you are carrying. I might go on and quote the next couplet too—
"'Kilmeny looked up with a lovely grace,
But there was nae smile on Kilmeny's face.'
"Why are you looking so sober?"

Kilmeny did not have her slate with her and could not answer; but Eric guessed from something in her eyes that she was bitterly contrasting the beauty of the ballad's heroine with her own supposed ugliness.

"Come down to the house, Kilmeny. I have something there to show you—something lovelier than you have ever seen before," he said, with boyish pleasure shining in his eyes. "I want you to go and put on that muslin dress you wore last Sunday evening, and pin up your hair the same way you did then. Run along—don't wait for me. But you are not to go into the parlour until I come. I want to pick some of those Mary-lilies up in the orchard."

When Eric returned to the house with an armful of the long stemmed, white Madonna lilies that bloomed in the orchard Kilmeny was just coming down the steep, narrow staircase with its striped carpeting of homespun drugget. Her marvelous loveliness was brought out into brilliant relief by the dark wood work and shadows of the dim old hall.

She wore a trailing, clinging dress of some creamy tinted fabric that had been her mother's. It had not been altered in any respect, for fashion held no sway at the Gordon homestead, and Kilmeny thought that the dress left nothing to be desired. Its quaint style suited her admirably; the neck was slightly cut away to show the round white throat, and the sleeves were long, full "bishops," out of which her beautiful, slender hands slipped like flowers from their sheaths. She had crossed her long braids at the back and pinned them about her head like a coronet; a late white rose was fastened low down on the left side.

"'A man had given all other bliss
And all his worldly wealth for this—
To waste his whole heart in one kiss
Upon her perfect lips,'"
quoted Eric in a whisper as he watched her descend. Aloud he said,

"Take these lilies on your arm, letting their bloom fall against your shoulder—so. Now, give me your hand and shut your eyes. Don't open them until I say you may."

He led her into the parlour and up to the mirror.

"Look," he cried, gaily.

Kilmeny opened her eyes and looked straight into the mirror where, like a lovely picture in a golden frame, she saw herself reflected. For a moment she was bewildered. Then she realized what it meant. The lilies fell from her arm to the floor and she turned pale. With a little low, involuntary cry she put her hands over her face.

Eric pulled them boyishly away.

"Kilmeny, do you think you are ugly now? This is a truer mirror than Aunt Janet's silver sugar bowl! Look—look—look! Did you ever imagine anything fairer than yourself, dainty Kilmeny?"

She was blushing now, and stealing shy radiant glances at the mirror. With a smile she took her slate and wrote naively,

"I think I am pleasant to look upon. I cannot tell you how glad I am. It is so dreadful to believe one is ugly. You can get used to everything else, but you never get used to that. It hurts just the same every time you remember it. But why did mother tell me I was ugly? Could she really have thought so? Perhaps I have become better looking since I grew up."

"I think perhaps your mother had found that beauty is not always a blessing, Kilmeny, and thought it wiser not to let you know you possessed it. Come, let us go back to the orchard now. We mustn't waste this rare evening in the house. There is going to be a sunset that we shall remember all our lives. The mirror will hang here. It is yours. Don't look into it too often, though, or Aunt Janet will disapprove. She is afraid it will make you vain."

Kilmeny gave one of her rare, musical laughs, which Eric never heard without a recurrence of the old wonder that she could laugh so when she could not speak. She blew an airy little kiss at her mirrored face and turned from it, smiling happily.

On their way to the orchard they met Neil. He went by them with an averted face, but Kilmeny shivered and involuntarily drew nearer to Eric.

"I don't understand Neil at all now," she wrote nervously. "He is not nice, as he used to be, and sometimes he will not answer when I speak to him. And he looks so strangely at me, too. Besides, he is surly and impertinent to Uncle and Aunt."

"Don't mind Neil," said Eric lightly. "He is probably sulky because of some things I said to him when I found he had spied on us."

That night before she went up stairs Kilmeny stole into the parlour for another glimpse of herself in that wonderful mirror by the light of a dim little candle she carried. She was still lingering there dreamily when Aunt Janet's grim face appeared in the shadows of the doorway.

"Are you thinking about your own good looks, lassie? Ay, but remember that handsome is as handsome does," she said, with grudging admiration— for the girl with her flushed cheeks and shining eyes was something that even dour Janet Gordon could not look upon unmoved.

Kilmeny smiled softly.

"I'll try to remember," she wrote, "but oh, Aunt Janet, I am so glad I am not ugly. It is not wrong to be glad of that, is it?"

The older woman's face softened.

"No, I don't suppose it is, lassie," she conceded. "A comely face is something to be thankful for—as none know better than those who have never possessed it. I remember well when I was a girl—but that is neither here nor there. The Master thinks you are wonderful bonny, Kilmeny," she added, looking keenly at the girl.

Kilmeny started and a scarlet blush scorched her face. That, and the expression that flashed into her eyes, told Janet Gordon all she wished to know. With a stifled sigh she bade her niece good night and went away.

Kilmeny ran fleetly up the stairs to her dim little room, that looked out into the spruces, and flung herself on her bed, burying her burning face in the pillow. Her aunt's words had revealed to her the hidden secret of her heart. She knew that she loved Eric Marshall—and the knowledge brought with it a strange anguish. For was she not dumb? All night she lay staring wide-eyed through the darkness till the dawn.

IN HER SELFLESS MOOD

Eric noticed a change in Kilmeny at their next meeting—a change that troubled him. She seemed aloof, abstracted, almost ill at ease. When he proposed an excursion to the orchard he thought she was reluctant to go. The days that followed convinced him of the change. Something had come between them. Kilmeny seemed as far away from him as if she had in truth, like her namesake of the ballad, sojourned for seven years in the land "where the rain never fell and the wind never blew," and had come back washed clean from all the affections of earth.

Eric had a bad week of it; but he determined to put an end to it by plain speaking. One evening in the orchard he told her of his love.

It was an evening in August, with wheat fields ripening to their harvestry—a soft violet night made for love, with the distant murmur of an unquiet sea on a rocky shore sounding through it. Kilmeny was sitting on the old bench where he had first seen her. She had been playing for him, but her music did not please her and she laid aside the violin with a little frown.

It might be that she was afraid to play—afraid that her new emotions might escape her and reveal themselves in music. It was difficult to prevent this, so long had she been accustomed to pour out all her feelings in harmony. The necessity for restraint irked her and made of her bow a clumsy thing which no longer obeyed her wishes. More than ever at that instant did she long for speech—speech that would conceal and protect where dangerous silence might betray.

In a low voice that trembled with earnestness Eric told her that he loved her—that he had loved her from the first time he had seen her in that old orchard. He spoke humbly but not fearfully, for he believed that she loved him, and he had little expectation of any rebuff.

"Kilmeny, will you be my wife?" he asked finally, taking her hands in his.

Kilmeny had listened with averted face. At first she had blushed painfully but now she had grown very pale. When he had finished speaking and was waiting for her answer, she suddenly pulled her hands away, and, putting them over her face, burst into tears and noiseless sobs.

"Kilmeny, dearest, have I alarmed you? Surely you knew before that I loved you. Don't you care for me?" Eric said, putting his arm about her and trying to draw her to him. But she shook her head sorrowfully, and wrote with compressed lips,

"Yes, I do love you, but I will never marry you, because I cannot speak."

"Oh, Kilmeny," said Eric smiling, for he believed his victory won, "that doesn't make any difference to me—you know it doesn't, sweetest. If you love me that is enough."

But Kilmeny only shook her head again. There was a very determined look on her pale face. She wrote,

"No, it is not enough. It would be doing you a great wrong to marry you when I cannot speak, and I will not do it because I love you too much to do anything that would harm you. Your world would think you had done a very foolish thing and it would be right. I have thought it all over many times since something Aunt Janet said made me understand, and I know I am doing right. I am sorry I did not understand sooner, before you had learned to care so much."

"Kilmeny, darling, you have taken a very absurd fancy into that dear black head of yours. Don't you know that you will make me miserably unhappy all my life if you will not be my wife?"

"No, you think so now; and I know you will feel very badly for a time. Then you will go away and after awhile you will forget me; and then you will see that I was right. I shall be very unhappy, too, but that is better than spoiling your life. Do not plead or coax because I shall not change my mind."

Eric did plead and coax, however—at first patiently and smilingly, as one might argue with a dear foolish child; then with vehement and distracted earnestness, as he began to realize that Kilmeny meant what she said. It was all in vain. Kilmeny grew paler and paler, and her eyes revealed how keenly she was suffering. She did not even try to argue with him, but only listened patiently and sadly, and shook her head. Say what he would, entreat and implore as he might, he could not move her resolution a hairs-breadth.

Yet he did not despair; he could not believe that she would adhere to such a resolution; he felt sure that her love for him would eventually conquer, and he went home not unhappily after all. He did not understand that it was the very intensity of her love which gave her the strength to resist his pleading, where a more shallow affection might have yielded. It held her back unflinchingly from doing him what she believed to be a wrong.

KILMENY OF THE ORCHARD

KILMENY OF THE ORCHARD

KILMENY OF THE ORCHARD

AN OLD, UNHAPPY, FAR-OFF THING

The next day Eric sought Kilmeny again and renewed his pleadings, but again in vain. Nothing he could say, no argument which he could advance, was of any avail against her sad determination. When he was finally compelled to realize that her resolution was not to be shaken, he went in his despair to Janet Gordon. Janet listened to his story with concern and disappointment plainly visible on her face. When he had finished she shook her head.

"I'm sorry, Master. I can't tell you how sorry I am. I had hoped for something very different. HOPED! I have PRAYED for it. Thomas and I are getting old and it has weighed on my mind for years—what was to become of Kilmeny when we would be gone. Since you came I had hoped she would have a protector in you. But if Kilmeny says she will not marry you I am afraid she'll stick to it."

"But she loves me," cried the young man, "and if you and her uncle speak to her—urge her—perhaps you can influence her—"

"No, Master, it wouldn't be any use. Oh, we will, of course, but it will not be any use. Kilmeny is as determined as her mother when once she makes up her mind. She has always been good and obedient for the most part, but once or twice we have found out that there is no moving her if she does resolve upon anything. When her mother died Thomas and I wanted to take her to church. We could not prevail on her to go. We did not know why then, but now I suppose it was because she believed she was so very ugly. It is because she thinks so much of you that she will not marry you. She is afraid you would come to repent having married a dumb girl. Maybe she is right—maybe she is right."

"I cannot give her up," said Eric stubbornly. "Something must be done. Perhaps her defect can be remedied even yet. Have you ever thought of

89

that? You have never had her examined by a doctor qualified to pronounce on her case, have you?"

"No, Master, we never took her to anyone. When we first began to fear that she was never going to talk Thomas wanted to take her to Charlottetown and have her looked to. He thought so much of the child and he felt terrible about it. But her mother wouldn't hear of it being done. There was no use trying to argue with her. She said that it would be no use—that it was her sin that was visited on her child and it could never be taken away."

"And did you give in meekly to a morbid whim like that?" asked Eric impatiently.

"Master, you didn't know my sister. We HAD to give in—nobody could hold out against her. She was a strange woman—and a terrible woman in many ways—after her trouble. We were afraid to cross her for fear she would go out of her mind."

"But, could you not have taken Kilmeny to a doctor unknown to her mother?"

"No, that was not possible. Margaret never let her out of her sight, not even when she was grown up. Besides, to tell you the whole truth, Master, we didn't think ourselves that it would be much use to try to cure Kilmeny. It WAS a sin that made her as she is."

"Aunt Janet, how can you talk such nonsense? Where was there any sin? Your sister thought herself a lawful wife. If Ronald Fraser thought otherwise—and there is no proof that he did—HE committed a sin, but you surely do not believe that it was visited in this fashion on his innocent child!"

"No, I am not meaning that, Master. That wasn't where Margaret did wrong; and though I never liked Ronald Fraser over much, I must say this in his defence—I believe he thought himself a free man when he married Margaret. No, it's something else—something far worse. It gives me a shiver whenever I think of it. Oh, Master, the Good Book is right when it says the sins of the parents are visited on the children. There isn't a truer word in it than that from cover to cover."

"What, in heaven's name, is the meaning of all this?" exclaimed Eric. "Tell me what it is. I must know the whole truth about Kilmeny. Do not torment me."

"I am going to tell you the story, Master, though it will be like opening an old wound. No living person knows it but Thomas and me. When you hear it you will understand why Kilmeny can't speak, and why it isn't likely that there can ever be anything done for her. She doesn't know the truth and you must never tell her. It isn't a fit story for her ears, especially when it is about her mother. Promise me that you will never tell her, no matter what may happen."

"I promise. Go on—go on," said the young man feverishly.

Janet Gordon locked her hands together in her lap, like a woman who nerves herself to some hateful task. She looked very old; the lines on her face seemed doubly deep and harsh.

"My sister Margaret was a very proud, high-spirited girl, Master. But I would not have you think she was unlovable. No, no, that would be doing a great injustice to her memory. She had her faults as we all have; but she was bright and merry and warm-hearted. We all loved her. She was the light and life of this house. Yes, Master, before the trouble that came on her Margaret was a winsome lass, singing like a lark from morning till night. Maybe we spoiled her a little—maybe we gave her too much of her own way.

"Well, Master, you have heard the story of her marriage to Ronald Fraser and what came after, so I need not go into that. I know, or used to know Elizabeth Williamson well, and I know that whatever she told you would be the truth and nothing more or less than the truth.

"Our father was a very proud man. Oh, Master, if Margaret was too proud she got it from no stranger. And her misfortune cut him to the heart. He never spoke a word to us here for more than three days after he heard of it. He sat in the corner there with bowed head and would not touch bite or sup. He had not been very willing for her to marry Ronald Fraser; and when she came home in disgrace she had not set foot over the threshold before he broke out railing at her. Oh, I can see her there at the door this very minute, Master, pale and trembling, clinging to Thomas's arm, her great eyes changing from sorrow and shame to wrath. It was just at sunset and a red ray came in at the window and fell right across her breast like a stain of blood.

"Father called her a hard name, Master. Oh, he was too hard—even though he was my father I must say he was too hard on her, broken-hearted as she was, and guilty of nothing more after all than a little willfulness in the matter of her marriage.

"And father was sorry for it—Oh, Master, the word wasn't out of his mouth before he was sorry for it. But the mischief was done. Oh, I'll never forget Margaret's face, Master! It haunts me yet in the black of the night. It was full of anger and rebellion and defiance. But she never answered him back. She clenched her hands and went up to her old room without saying a word, all those mad feelings surging in her soul, and being held back from speech by her sheer, stubborn will. And, Master, never a word did Margaret say from that day until after Kilmeny was born—not one word, Master. Nothing we could do for her softened her. And we were kind to her, Master, and gentle with her, and never reproached her by so much as a look. But she would not speak to anyone. She just sat in her room most of the time and stared at the wall with such awful eyes. Father implored her to speak and forgive him, but she never gave any sign that she heard him.

"I haven't come to the worst yet, Master. Father sickened and took to his bed. Margaret would not go in to see him. Then one night Thomas and I were watching by him; it was about eleven o'clock. All at once he said,

"'Janet, go up and tell the lass'—he always called Margaret that—it was a kind of pet name he had for her—'that I'm deein' and ask her to come down and speak to me afore I'm gone.'

"Master, I went. Margaret was sitting in her room all alone in the cold and dark, staring at the wall. I told her what our father had said. She never let on she heard me. I pleaded and wept, Master. I did what I had never done to any human creature—I kneeled to her and begged her, as she hoped for mercy herself, to come down and see our dying father. Master, she wouldn't! She never moved or looked at me. I had to get up and go downstairs and tell that old man she would not come."

Janet Gordon lifted her hands and struck them together in her agony of remembrance.

"When I told father he only said, oh, so gently,

"'Poor lass, I was too hard on her. She isna to blame. But I canna go to meet her mother till our little lass has forgie'n me for the name I called her. Thomas, help me up. Since she winna come to me I must e'en go to her.'

"There was no crossing him—we saw that. He got up from his deathbed and Thomas helped him out into the hall and up the stair. I walked behind with the candle. Oh, Master, I'll never forget it—the awful shadows and the storm wind wailing outside, and father's gasping breath. But we got him to Margaret's room and he stood before her, trembling, with his white hairs falling about his sunken face. And he prayed Margaret to forgive him—to forgive him and speak just one word to him before he went to meet her mother. Master"—Janet's voice rose almost to a shriek—"she would not— she would not! And yet she WANTED to speak—afterwards she confessed to me that she wanted to speak. But her stubbornness wouldn't let her. It was like some evil power that had gripped hold of her and wouldn't let go. Father might as well have pleaded with a graven image. Oh, it was hard and dreadful! She saw her father die and she never spoke the word he prayed for to him. THAT was her sin, Master,—and for that sin the curse fell on her unborn child. When father understood that she would not speak he closed his eyes and was like to have fallen if Thomas had not caught him.

"'Oh, lass, you're a hard woman,' was all he said. And they were his last words. Thomas and I carried him back to his room, but the breath was gone from him before we ever got him there.

"Well, Master, Kilmeny was born a month afterwards, and when Margaret felt her baby at her breast the evil thing that had held her soul in its bondage lost its power. She spoke and wept and was herself again. Oh, how she wept! She implored us to forgive her and we did freely and fully. But the one against whom she had sinned most grievously was gone, and no word of forgiveness could come to her from the grave. My poor sister never knew peace of conscience again, Master. But she was gentle and kind and humble until—until she began to fear that Kilmeny was never going to speak. We thought then that she would go out of her mind. Indeed, Master, she never was quite right again.

"But that is the story and it's a thankful woman I am that the telling of it is done. Kilmeny can't speak because her mother wouldn't."

Eric had listened with a gray horror on his face to the gruesome tale. The black tragedy of it appalled him—the tragedy of that merciless law, the most cruel and mysterious thing in God's universe, which ordains that the sin of the guilty shall be visited on the innocent. Fight against it as he would, the miserable conviction stole into his heart that Kilmeny's case was indeed beyond the reach of any human skill.

"It is a dreadful tale," he said moodily, getting up and walking restlessly to and fro in the dim spruce-shadowed old kitchen where they were. "And if it is true that her mother's willful silence caused Kilmeny's dumbness, I fear, as you say, that we cannot help her. But you may be mistaken. It may have been nothing more than a strange coincidence. Possibly something may be done for her. At all events, we must try. I have a friend in Queenslea who is a physician. His name is David Baker, and he is a very skilful specialist in regard to the throat and voice. I shall have him come here and see Kilmeny."

"Have your way," assented Janet in the hopeless tone which she might have used in giving him permission to attempt any impossible thing.

"It will be necessary to tell Dr. Baker why Kilmeny cannot speak—or why you think she cannot."

Janet's face twitched.

"Must that be, Master? Oh, it's a bitter tale to tell a stranger."

"Don't be afraid. I shall tell him nothing that is not strictly necessary to his proper understanding of the case. It will be quite enough to say that Kilmeny may be dumb because for several months before her birth her mother's mind was in a very morbid condition, and she preserved a stubborn and unbroken silence because of a certain bitter personal resentment."

"Well, do as you think best, Master."

Janet plainly had no faith in the possibility of anything being done for Kilmeny. But a rosy glow of hope flashed over Kilmeny's face when Eric told her what he meant to do.

"Oh, do you think he can make me speak?" she wrote eagerly.

"I don't know, Kilmeny. I hope that he can, and I know he will do all that mortal skill can do. If he can remove your defect will you promise to marry me, dearest?"

She nodded. The grave little motion had the solemnity of a sacred promise.

"Yes," she wrote, "when I can speak like other women I will marry you."

DAVID BAKER'S OPINION

The next week David Baker came to Lindsay. He arrived in the afternoon when Eric was in school. When the latter came home he found that David had, in the space of an hour, captured Mrs. Williamson's heart, wormed himself into the good graces of Timothy, and become hail-fellow-well-met with old Robert. But he looked curiously at Eric when the two young men found themselves alone in the upstairs room.

"Now, Eric, I want to know what all this is about. What scrape have you got into? You write me a letter, entreating me in the name of friendship to come to you at once. Accordingly I come post haste. You seem to be in excellent health yourself. Explain why you have inveigled me hither."

"I want you to do me a service which only you can do, David," said Eric quietly. "I didn't care to go into the details by letter. I have met in Lindsay a young girl whom I have learned to love. I have asked her to marry me, but, although she cares for me, she refuses to do so because she is dumb. I wish you to examine her and find out the cause of her defect, and if it can be cured. She can hear perfectly and all her other faculties are entirely normal. In order that you may better understand the case I must tell you the main facts of her history."

This Eric proceeded to do. David Baker listened with grave attention, his eyes fastened on his friend's face. He did not betray the surprise and dismay he felt at learning that Eric had fallen in love with a dumb girl of doubtful antecedents; and the strange case enlisted his professional interest. When he had heard the whole story he thrust his hands into his pockets and strode up and down the room several times in silence. Finally he halted before Eric.

"So you have done what I foreboded all along you would do—left your common sense behind you when you went courting."

95

"If I did," said Eric quietly, "I took with me something better and nobler than common sense."

David shrugged his shoulders.

"You'll have hard work to convince me of that, Eric."

"No, it will not be difficult at all. I have one argument that will convince you speedily—and that is Kilmeny Gordon herself. But we will not discuss the matter of my wisdom or lack of it just now. What I want to know is this—what do you think of the case as I have stated it to you?"

David frowned thoughtfully.

"I hardly know what to think. It is very curious and unusual, but it is not totally unprecedented. There have been cases on record where pre-natal influences have produced a like result. I cannot just now remember whether any were ever cured. Well, I'll see if anything can be done for this girl. I cannot express any further opinion until I have examined her."

The next morning Eric took David up to the Gordon homestead. As they approached the old orchard a strain of music came floating through the resinous morning arcades of the spruce wood—a wild, sorrowful, appealing cry, full of indescribable pathos, yet marvelously sweet.

"What is that?" exclaimed David, starting.

"That is Kilmeny playing on her violin," answered Eric. "She has great talent in that respect and improvises wonderful melodies."

When they reached the orchard Kilmeny rose from the old bench to meet them, her lovely luminous eyes distended, her face flushed with the excitement of mingled hope and fear.

"Oh, ye gods!" muttered David helplessly.

He could not hide his amazement and Eric smiled to see it. The latter had not failed to perceive that his friend had until now considered him as little better than a lunatic.

"Kilmeny, this is my friend, Dr. Baker," he said.

Kilmeny held out her hand with a smile. Her beauty, as she stood there in the fresh morning sunshine beside a clump of her sister lilies, was something to take away a man's breath. David, who was by no means lacking in confidence and generally had a ready tongue where women were concerned, found himself as mute and awkward as a school boy, as he bowed over her hand.

But Kilmeny was charmingly at ease. There not a trace of embarrassment in her manner, though there was a pretty shyness. Eric smiled as he recalled HIS first meeting with her. He suddenly realized how far Kilmeny had come since then and how much she had developed.

With a little gesture of invitation Kilmeny led the way through the orchard to the wild cherry lane, and the two men followed.

"Eric, she is simply unutterable!" said David in an undertone. "Last night, to tell you the truth, I had a rather poor opinion of your sanity. But now I am consumed with a fierce envy. She is the loveliest creature I ever saw."

Eric introduced David to the Gordons and then hurried away to his school. On his way down the Gordon lane he met Neil and was half startled by the glare of hatred in the Italian boy's eyes. Pity succeeded the momentary alarm. Neil's face had grown thin and haggard; his eyes were sunken and feverishly bright; he looked years older than on the day when Eric had first seen him in the brook hollow.

Prompted by sudden compassionate impulse Eric stopped and held out his hand.

"Neil, can't we be friends?" he said. "I am sorry if I have been the cause of inflicting pain on you."

"Friends! Never!" said Neil passionately. "You have taken Kilmeny from me. I shall hate you always. And I'll be even with you yet."

He strode fiercely up the lane, and Eric, with a shrug of his shoulders, went on his way, dismissing the meeting from his mind.

The day seemed interminably long to him. David had not returned when he went home to dinner; but when he went to his room in the evening he found his friend there, staring out of the window.

"Well," he said, impatiently, as David wheeled around but still kept silence, "What have you to say to me? Don't keep me in suspense any longer, David. I have endured all I can. To-day has seemed like a thousand years. Have you discovered what is the matter with Kilmeny?"

"There is nothing the matter with her," answered David slowly, flinging himself into a chair by the window.

"What do you mean?"

"Just exactly what I say. Her vocal organs are all perfect. As far as they are concerned, there is absolutely no reason why she should not speak."

"Then why can't she speak? Do you think—do you think—"

"I think that I cannot express my conclusion in any better words than Janet Gordon used when she said that Kilmeny cannot speak because her mother wouldn't. That is all there is to it. The trouble is psychological, not physical. Medical skill is helpless before it. There are greater men than I in my profession; but it is my honest belief, Eric, that if you were to consult them they would tell you just what I have told you, neither more nor less."

"Then there is no hope," said Eric in a tone of despair. "You can do nothing for her?"

David took from the back of his chair a crochet antimacassar with a lion rampant in the center and spread it over his knee.

"I can do nothing for her," he said, scowling at that work of art. "I do not believe any living man can do anything for her. But I do not say—exactly— that there is no hope."

"Come, David, I am in no mood for guessing riddles. Speak plainly, man, and don't torment me."

David frowned dubiously and poked his finger through the hole which represented the eye of the king of beasts.

"I don't know that I can make it plain to you. It isn't very plain to myself. And it is only a vague theory of mine, of course. I cannot substantiate it by any facts. In short, Eric, I think it is possible that Kilmeny may speak sometime—if she ever wants it badly enough."

"Wants to! Why, man, she wants to as badly as it is possible for any one to want anything. She loves me with all her heart and she won't marry me because she can't speak. Don't you suppose that a girl under such circumstances would 'want' to speak as much as any one could?"

"Yes, but I do not mean that sort of wanting, no matter how strong the wish may be. What I do mean is—a sudden, vehement, passionate inrush of desire, physical, psychical, mental, all in one, mighty enough to rend asunder the invisible fetters that hold her speech in bondage. If any occasion should arise to evoke such a desire I believe that Kilmeny would speak—and having once spoken would thenceforth be normal in that respect—ay, if she spoke but the one word."

"All this sounds like great nonsense to me," said Eric restlessly. "I suppose you have an idea what you are talking about, but I haven't. And, in any case, it practically means that there is no hope for her—or me. Even if your theory is correct it is not likely such an occasion as you speak of will ever arise. And Kilmeny will never marry me."

"Don't give up so easily, old fellow. There HAVE been cases on record where women have changed their minds."

"Not women like Kilmeny," said Eric miserably. "I tell you she has all her mother's unfaltering will and tenacity of purpose, although she is free from any taint of pride or selfishness. I thank you for your sympathy and interest, David. You have done all you could—but, heavens, what it would have meant to me if you could have helped her!"

With a groan Eric flung himself on a chair and buried his face in his hands. It was a moment which held for him all the bitterness of death. He had thought that he was prepared for disappointment; he had not known how strong his hope had really been until that hope was utterly taken from him.

David, with a sigh, returned the crochet antimacassar carefully to its place on the chair back.

"Eric, last night, to be honest, I thought that, if I found I could not help this girl, it would be the best thing that could happen, as far as you were concerned. But since I have seen her—well, I would give my right hand if I could do anything for her. She is the wife for you, if we could make her speak; yes, and by the memory of your mother"—David brought his fist down on the window sill with a force that shook the casement,—"she is the wife for you, speech or no speech, if we could only convince her of it."

"She cannot be convinced of that. No, David, I have lost her. Did you tell her what you have told me?"

"I told her I could not help her. I did not say anything to her of my theory—that would have done no good."

"How did she take it?"

"Very bravely and quietly—'like a winsome lady'. But the look in her eyes— Eric, I felt as if I had murdered something. She bade me good-bye with a pitiful smile and went upstairs. I did not see her again, although I stayed to dinner as her uncle's request. Those old Gordons are a queer pair. I liked them, though. They are strong and staunch—good friends, bitter enemies. They were sorry that I could not help Kilmeny, but I saw plainly that old Thomas Gordon thought that I had been meddling with predestination in attempting it."

Eric smiled mechanically.

"I must go up and see Kilmeny. You'll excuse me, won't you, David? My books are there—help yourself."

But when Eric reached the Gordon house he saw only old Janet, who told him that Kilmeny was in her room and refused to see him.

"She thought you would come up, and she left this with me to give you, Master."

Janet handed him a little note. It was very brief and blotted with tears.

"Do not come any more, Eric," it ran. "I must not see you, because it would only make it harder for us both. You must go away and forget me. You will be thankful for this some day. I shall always love and pray for you."

    "KILMENY."

"I MUST see her," said Eric desperately. "Aunt Janet, be my friend. Tell her she must see me for a little while at least."

Janet shook her head but went upstairs. She soon returned.

"She says she cannot come down. You know she means it, Master, and it is of no use to coax her. And I must say I think she is right. Since she will not marry you it is better for her not to see you."

Eric was compelled to go home with no better comfort than this. In the morning, as it was Sunday, he drove David Baker to the station. He had not slept and he looked so miserable and reckless that David felt anxious about him. David would have stayed in Lindsay for a few days, but a certain critical case in Queenslea demanded his speedy return. He shook hands with Eric on the station platform.

"Eric, give up that school and come home at once. You can do no good in Lindsay now, and you'll only eat your heart out here."

"I must see Kilmeny once more before I leave," was all Eric's answer.

That afternoon he went again to the Gordon homestead. But the result was the same; Kilmeny refused to see him, and Thomas Gordon said gravely,

"Master, you know I like you and I am sorry Kilmeny thinks as she does, though maybe she is right. I would be glad to see you often for your own sake and I'll miss you much; but as things are I tell you plainly you'd better not come here any more. It will do no good, and the sooner you and she get over thinking about each other the better for you both. Go now, lad, and God bless you."

"Do you know what it is you are asking of me?" said Eric hoarsely.

"I know I am asking a hard thing for your own good, Master. It is not as if Kilmeny would ever change her mind. We have had some experience with a woman's will ere this. Tush, Janet, woman, don't be weeping. You women are foolish creatures. Do you think tears can wash such things away? No, they cannot blot out sin, or the consequences of sin. It's awful how one sin can spread out and broaden, till it eats into innocent lives, sometimes long after the sinner has gone to his own accounting. Master, if you take my advice, you'll give up the Lindsay school and go back to your own world as soon as may be."

A BROKEN FETTER

Eric went home with a white, haggard face. He had never thought it was possible for a man to suffer as he suffered then. What was he to do? It seemed impossible to go on with life—there was NO life apart from Kilmeny. Anguish wrung his soul until his strength went from him and youth and hope turned to gall and bitterness in his heart.

He never afterwards could tell how he lived through the following Sunday or how he taught school as usual on Monday. He found out how much a man may suffer and yet go on living and working. His body seemed to him an automaton that moved and spoke mechanically, while his tortured spirit, pent-up within, endured pain that left its impress on him for ever. Out of that fiery furnace of agony Eric Marshall was to go forth a man who had put boyhood behind him for ever and looked out on life with eyes that saw into it and beyond.

On Tuesday afternoon there was a funeral in the district and, according to custom, the school was closed. Eric went again to the old orchard. He had no expectation of seeing Kilmeny there, for he thought she would avoid the spot lest she might meet him. But he could not keep away from it, although the thought of it was an added torment, and he vibrated between a wild wish that he might never see it again, and a sick wonder how he could possibly go away and leave it—that strange old orchard where he had met and wooed his sweetheart, watching her develop and blossom under his eyes, like some rare flower, until in the space of three short months she had passed from exquisite childhood into still more exquisite womanhood.

As he crossed the pasture field before the spruce wood he came upon Neil Gordon, building a longer fence. Neil did not look up as Eric passed, but sullenly went on driving poles. Before this Eric had pitied Neil; now he was conscious of feeling sympathy with him. Had Neil suffered as he was suffering? Eric had entered into a new fellowship whereof the passport was pain.

The orchard was very silent and dreamy in the thick, deep tinted sunshine of the September afternoon, a sunshine which seemed to possess the power of extracting the very essence of all the odours which summer has stored up in wood and field. There were few flowers now; most of the lilies, which had queened it so bravely along the central path a few days before, were withered. The grass had become ragged and sere and unkempt. But in the corners the torches of the goldenrod were kindling and a few misty purple asters nodded here and there. The orchard kept its own strange attractiveness, as some women with youth long passed still preserve an atmosphere of remembered beauty and innate, indestructible charm.

Eric walked drearily and carelessly about it, and finally sat down on a half fallen fence panel in the shadow of the overhanging spruce boughs. There he gave himself up to a reverie, poignant and bitter sweet, in which he lived over again everything that had passed in the orchard since his first meeting there with Kilmeny.

So deep was his abstraction that he was conscious of nothing around him. He did not hear stealthy footsteps behind him in the dim spruce wood. He did not even see Kilmeny as she came slowly around the curve of the wild cherry lane.

Kilmeny had sought the old orchard for the healing of her heartbreak, if healing were possible for her. She had no fear of encountering Eric there at that time of day, for she did not know that it was the district custom to close the school for a funeral. She would never have gone to it in the evening, but she longed for it continually; it, and her memories, were all that was left her now.

Years seemed to have passed over the girl in those few days. She had drunk of pain and broken bread with sorrow. Her face was pale and strained, with bluish, transparent shadows under her large wistful eyes, out of which the dream and laughter of girlhood had gone, but into which had come the potent charm of grief and patience. Thomas Gordon had shaken his head bodingly when he had looked at her that morning at the breakfast table.

"She won't stand it," he thought. "She isn't long for this world. Maybe it is all for the best, poor lass. But I wish that young Master had never set foot in the Connors orchard, or in this house. Margaret, Margaret, it's hard that your child should have to be paying the reckoning of a sin that was sinned before her birth."

Kilmeny walked through the lane slowly and absently like a woman in a dream. When she came to the gap in the fence where the lane ran into the orchard she lifted her wan, drooping face and saw Eric, sitting in the shadow of the wood at the other side of the orchard with his bowed head in his hands. She stopped quickly and the blood rushed wildly over her face.

The next moment it ebbed, leaving her white as marble. Horror filled her eyes,—blank, deadly horror, as the livid shadow of a cloud might fill two blue pools.

Behind Eric Neil Gordon was standing tense, crouched, murderous. Even at that distance Kilmeny saw the look on his face, saw what he held in his hand, and realized in one agonized flash of comprehension what it meant.

All this photographed itself in her brain in an instant. She knew that by the time she could run across the orchard to warn Eric by a touch it would be too late. Yet she must warn him—she MUST—she MUST! A mighty surge of desire seemed to rise up within her and overwhelm her like a wave of the sea,—a surge that swept everything before it in an irresistible flood. As Neil Gordon swiftly and vindictively, with the face of a demon, lifted the axe he held in his hand, Kilmeny sprang forward through the gap.

"ERIC, ERIC, LOOK BEHIND YOU—LOOK BEHIND YOU!"

Eric started up, confused, bewildered, as the voice came shrieking across the orchard. He did not in the least realize that it was Kilmeny who had called to him, but he instinctively obeyed the command.

He wheeled around and saw Neil Gordon, who was looking, not at him, but past him at Kilmeny. The Italian boy's face was ashen and his eyes were filled with terror and incredulity, as if he had been checked in his murderous purpose by some supernatural interposition. The axe, lying at his feet where he had dropped it in his unutterable consternation on hearing Kilmeny's cry told the whole tale. But before Eric could utter a word Neil turned, with a cry more like that of an animal than a human being, and fled like a hunted creature into the shadow of the spruce wood.

A moment later Kilmeny, her lovely face dewed with tears and sunned over with smiles, flung herself on Eric's breast.

"Oh, Eric, I can speak,—I can speak! Oh, it is so wonderful! Eric, I love you—I love you!"

NEIL GORDON SOLVES HIS OWN PROBLEM

"It is a miracle!" said Thomas Gordon in an awed tone.

It was the first time he had spoken since Eric and Kilmeny had rushed in, hand in hand, like two children intoxicated with joy and wonder, and gasped out their story together to him and Janet.

"Oh, no, it is very wonderful, but it is not a miracle," said Eric. "David told me it might happen. I had no hope that it would. He could explain it all to you if he were here."

Thomas Gordon shook his head. "I doubt if he could, Master—he, or any one else. It is near enough to a miracle for me. Let us thank God reverently and humbly that he has seen fit to remove his curse from the innocent. Your doctors may explain it as they like, lad, but I'm thinking they won't get much nearer to it than that. It is awesome, that is what it is. Janet, woman, I feel as if I were in a dream. Can Kilmeny really speak?"

"Indeed I can, Uncle," said Kilmeny, with a rapturous glance at Eric. "Oh, I don't know how it came to me—I felt that I MUST speak—and I did. And it is so easy now—it seems to me as if I could always have done it."

She spoke naturally and easily. The only difficulty which she seemed to experience was in the proper modulation of her voice. Occasionally she pitched it too high—again, too low. But it was evident that she would soon acquire perfect control of it. It was a beautiful voice—very clear and soft and musical.

"Oh, I am so glad that the first word I said was your name, dearest," she murmured to Eric.

"What about Neil?" asked Thomas Gordon gravely, rousing himself with an effort from his abstraction of wonder. "What are we to do with him when he returns? In one way this is a sad business."

Eric had almost forgotten about Neil in his overwhelming amazement and

105

joy. The realization of his escape from sudden and violent death had not yet had any opportunity to take possession of his thoughts.

"We must forgive him, Mr. Gordon. I know how I should feel towards a man who took Kilmeny from me. It was an evil impulse to which he gave way in his suffering—and think of the good which has resulted from it."

"That is true, Master, but it does not alter the terrible fact that the boy had murder in his heart,—that he would have killed you. An over-ruling Providence has saved him from the actual commission of the crime and brought good out of evil; but he is guilty in thought and purpose. And we have cared for him and instructed him as our own—with all his faults we have loved him! It is a hard thing, and I do not see what we are to do. We cannot act as if nothing had happened. We can never trust him again."

But Neil Gordon solved the problem himself. When Eric returned that night he found old Robert Williamson in the pantry regaling himself with a lunch of bread and cheese after a trip to the station. Timothy sat on the dresser in black velvet state and gravely addressed himself to the disposal of various tid-bits that came his way.

"Good night, Master. Glad to see you're looking more like yourself. I told the wife it was only a lover's quarrel most like. She's been worrying about you; but she didn't like to ask you what was the trouble. She ain't one of them unfortunate folks who can't be happy athout they're everlasting poking their noses into other people's business. But what kind of a rumpus was kicked up at the Gordon place, to-night, Master?"

Eric looked amazed. What could Robert Williamson have heard so soon?

"What do you mean?" he asked.

"Why, us folks at the station knew there must have been a to-do of some kind when Neil Gordon went off on the harvest excursion the way he did."

"Neil gone! On the harvest excursion!" exclaimed Eric.

"Yes, sir. You know this was the night the excursion train left. They cross on the boat to-night—special trip. There was a dozen or so fellows from hereabouts went. We was all standing around chatting when Lincoln Frame drove up full speed and Neil jumped out of his rig. Just bolted into the office, got his ticket and out again, and on to the train without a word to any one, and as black looking as the Old Scratch himself. We was all too surprised to speak till he was gone. Lincoln couldn't give us much information. He said Neil had rushed up to their place about dark, looking as if the constable was after him, and offered to sell that black filly of his to Lincoln for sixty dollars if Lincoln would drive him to the station in time to catch the excursion train. The filly was Neil's own, and Lincoln had been wanting to buy her but Neil would never hear to it afore. Lincoln jumped at the chance. Neil had brought the filly with him, and Lincoln hitched right up and took him to the station. Neil hadn't no luggage of any kind and wouldn't open his mouth the whole way up, Lincoln says. We concluded him and old Thomas must have had a row. D'ye know anything about it? Or was you so wrapped up in sweethearting that you didn't hear or see nothing else?"

Eric reflected rapidly. He was greatly relieved to find that Neil had gone. He would never return and this was best for all concerned. Old Robert must be told a part of the truth at least, since it would soon become known that Kilmeny could speak.

"There was some trouble at the Gordon place to-night, Mr. Williamson," he said quietly. "Neil Gordon behaved rather badly and frightened Kilmeny terribly,—so terribly that a very surprising thing has happened. She has found herself able to speak, and can speak perfectly."

Old Robert laid down the piece of cheese he was conveying to his mouth on the point of a knife and stared at Eric in blank amazement.

"God bless my soul, Master, what an extraordinary thing!" he ejaculated. "Are you in earnest? Or are you trying to see how much of a fool you can make of the old man?"

"No, Mr. Williamson, I assure you it is no more than the simple truth. Dr. Baker told me that a shock might cure her,—and it has. As for Neil, he has gone, no doubt for good, and I think it well that he has."

Not caring to discuss the matter further, Eric left the kitchen. But as he mounted the stairs to his room he heard old Robert muttering, like a man in hopeless bewilderment,

"Well, I never heard anything like this in all my born days—never—never. Timothy, did YOU ever hear the like? Them Gordons are an unaccountable lot and no mistake. They couldn't act like other people if they tried. I must wake mother up and tell her about this, or I'll never be able to sleep."

VICTOR FROM VANQUISHED ISSUES

Now that everything was settled Eric wished to give up teaching and go back to his own place. True, he had "signed papers" to teach the school for a year; but he knew that the trustees would let him off if he procured a suitable substitute. He resolved to teach until the fall vacation, which came in October, and then go. Kilmeny had promised that their marriage should take place in the following spring. Eric had pleaded for an earlier date, but Kilmeny was sweetly resolute, and Thomas and Janet agreed with her.

"There are so many things that I must learn yet before I shall be ready to be married," Kilmeny had said. "And I want to get accustomed to seeing people. I feel a little frightened yet whenever I see any one I don't know, although I don't think I show it. I am going to church with Uncle and Aunt after this, and to the Missionary Society meetings. And Uncle Thomas says that he will send me to a boarding school in town this winter if you think it advisable."

Eric vetoed this promptly. The idea of Kilmeny in a boarding school was something that could not be thought about without laughter.

"I can't see why she can't learn all she needs to learn after she is married to me, just as well as before," he grumbled to her uncle and aunt.

"But we want to keep her with us for another winter yet," explained Thomas Gordon patiently. "We are going to miss her terrible when she does go, Master. She has never been away from us for a day—she is all the brightness there is in our lives. It is very kind of you to say that she can come home whenever she likes, but there will be a great difference. She will belong to your world and not to ours. That is for the best—and we wouldn't have it otherwise. But let us keep her as our own for this one winter yet."

Eric yielded with the best grace he could muster. After all, he reflected,

Lindsay was not so far from Queenslea, and there were such things as boats and trains.

"Have you told your father about all this yet?" asked Janet anxiously.

No, he had not. But he went home and wrote a full account of his summer to old Mr. Marshall that night.

Mr. Marshall, Senior, answered the letter in person. A few days later, Eric, coming home from school, found his father sitting in Mrs. Williamson's prim, fleckless parlour. Nothing was said about Eric's letter, however, until after tea. When they found themselves alone, Mr. Marshall said abruptly,

"Eric, what about this girl? I hope you haven't gone and made a fool of yourself. It sounds remarkably like it. A girl that has been dumb all her life—a girl with no right to her father's name—a country girl brought up in a place like Lindsay! Your wife will have to fill your mother's place,—and your mother was a pearl among women. Do you think this girl is worthy of it? It isn't possible! You've been led away by a pretty face and dairy maid freshness. I expected some trouble out of this freak of yours coming over here to teach school."

"Wait until you see Kilmeny, father," said Eric, smiling.

"Humph! That's just exactly what David Baker said. I went straight to him when I got your letter, for I knew that there was some connection between it and that mysterious visit of his over here, concerning which I never could drag a word out of him by hook or crook. And all HE said was, 'Wait until you see Kilmeny Gordon, sir.' Well, I WILL wait till I see her, but I shall look at her with the eyes of sixty-five, mind you, not the eyes of twenty-four. And if she isn't what your wife ought to be, sir, you give her up or paddle your own canoe. I shall not aid or abet you in making a fool of yourself and spoiling your life."

Eric bit his lip, but only said quietly,

"Come with me, father. We will go to see her now."

They went around by way of the main road and the Gordon lane. Kilmeny was not in when they reached the house.

"She is up in the old orchard, Master," said Janet. "She loves that place so much she spends all her spare time there. She likes to go there to study."

They sat down and talked awhile with Thomas and Janet. When they left, Mr. Marshall said,

"I like those people. If Thomas Gordon had been a man like Robert Williamson I shouldn't have waited to see your Kilmeny. But they are all right—rugged and grim, but of good stock and pith—native refinement and strong character. But I must say candidly that I hope your young lady hasn't got her aunt's mouth."

"Kilmeny's mouth is like a love-song made incarnate in sweet flesh," said Eric enthusiastically.

"Humph!" said Mr. Marshall. "Well," he added more tolerantly, a moment later, "I was a poet, too, for six months in my life when I was courting your mother."

Kilmeny was reading on the bench under the lilac trees when they reached the orchard. She stood up and came shyly forward to meet them, guessing who the tall, white-haired old gentleman with Eric must be. As she approached Eric saw with a thrill of exultation that she had never looked lovelier. She wore a dress of her favourite blue, simply and quaintly made, as all her gowns were, revealing the perfect lines of her lithe, slender figure. Her glossy black hair was wound about her head in a braided coronet, against which a spray of wild asters shone like pale purple stars. Her face was flushed delicately with excitement. She looked like a young princess, crowned with a ruddy splash of sunlight that fell through the old trees.

"Father, this is Kilmeny," said Eric proudly.

Kilmeny held out her hand with a shyly murmured greeting. Mr. Marshall took it and held it in his, looking so steadily and piercingly into her face that even her frank gaze wavered before the intensity of his keen old eyes. Then he drew her to him and kissed her gravely and gently on her white forehead. "My dear," he said, "I am glad and proud that you have consented to be my son's wife—and my very dear and honoured daughter."

Eric turned abruptly away to hide his emotion and on his face was a light as of one who sees a great glory widening and deepening down the vista of his future.

THE END

CPSIA information can be obtained
at www.ICGtesting.com
Printed in the USA
BVOW09s1500141216
470814BV00012BA/200/P